CROSSINGS

CROSSINGS

Chuang Hua

With an Afterword by Amy Ling

 A NEW DIRECTIONS CLASSIC

Crossings was first published in 1968 by The Dial Press, and
reprinted by Northeastern University Press in 1986. This
New Directions Classic edition is published by arrangement
with Chuang Hua's daughter, Theodora Copley.

Manufactured in the United States of America
New Directions Books are printed on acid-free paper
First published as a New Directions Paperbook (NDP1076)
in 2007
Published simultaneously in Canada by Penguin Books
Canada Limited

Library of Congress Cataloging-in-Publication Data

Chuang, Hua.
  Crossings / Chuang Hua ; with an afterword by Amy Ling.
    p. cm. — (A New Directions Classic)
  ISBN 978-0-8112-1668-5 (acid-free paper)
  1. Chinese American women—Fiction. 2. Chinese
American families—Fiction.
I. Title.
PS3553.H78C7 2007
813'.54—dc22

                                2007010330

New Directions Books are published for James Laughlin
by New Directions Publishing Corporation
80 Eighth Avenue, New York, NY 10011

CROSSINGS

*S*he glanced at her watch, a round gold face with thin round numerals which Dyadya had bought on a holiday in Geneva the summer of 1938. He had several times worn out and changed the straps before putting it away as too outmoded. Fifth James was asked to choose from the collection. He took the large plain one in stainless steel that was supposed to be worn on a chain. Sixth Michael did not want a memento. She had chosen this one out of all the other accumulated time pieces heaped in the bottom of a shabby loose-hinged jewel case which Ngmah had found in a drawer of the filing cabinet in the study next to his bedroom. She remembered having seen him winding it, thoughtfully slowing down toward the final wind.

She was waiting on a pale sunlit street for a bus that she hoped would bring her to the other side of the city and deposit her within walking distance of her appointment. She had checked in the guidebook before leaving her hotel room and had found two buses which might bring her close enough—the 82 and the 83. After waiting a few minutes there was no sign of the bus. She decided to take a chance on the bus' not appearing for the moment and crossed the empty street to buy a pack of cigarettes in a tobacco shop.

He was watching her while she recrossed the street, thoughtful and on guard, his hands in the pockets of his short ash-colored raincoat. She retreated both from his glance and from the bus stop where he was also waiting, and found shelter under a tiny shop awning. There she took out the guidebook from her bag to reassure herself of the route.

Her appointment was to be in twenty minutes. In a moment of doubt she wondered if the routes had been changed since the last printing of the guidebook. Had a taxi passed by at that moment she would have hailed it. Once more she took out the guidebook from her handbag.

Their glances met when she looked up. He was still watching her in the same guarded and thoughtful way and this time she did not avoid his eyes.

Does one wait here for the bus to the Square?

The Square was not precisely where she had intended to get off but was near enough, judging by the map, so she said Square to simplify her question in a language she was not yet accustomed to.

Yes.

She hesitated.

Yes, they all go to the Square. The runs are few this time of year. Summer schedule. What part of the Square do you want to go to? It's fairly large you know.

Well I really don't want the Square I want to go to the Boulevard.

Oh, that's altogether a different problem. Furthermore it all depends on the number you want. It's a long boulevard. Here, give me your guidebook. I think it's either the 82 or the 83.

He took her guidebook. While he was leafing through an 83 lumbered into view and came to a lurching halt at the stop. He shook his head.

No, not that one.

Passengers got off. In a clang of bells and sputtering motor, the bus made off down the street. He looked up from the guidebook.

Damn. I do believe that was the bus you should have taken after all.

Yes, I thought it might have been the 83.

You're right. The trouble is there won't be another one coming for a while. Summer schedule. What time do you have to be there?

I have a dentist appointment at ten-thirty.

A taxi. You shall have to take a taxi.

I think there's a stand around the corner. Good-bye. Thank you for trying to help.

We'll take a taxi together. I'll drop you since I am going the same way.

Where are you going?

To the Circle.

But I'm going much farther. Why don't you let me drop you?

No. It was my fault you missed the bus. Besides you have an appointment.

Grasping her arm, he guided her quickly and firmly across the street to a taxi stand just around the corner. There weren't any parked in line. He held her arm above the elbow while scanning the traffic moving along the avenue. A taxi finally pulled up at the curb and splashed them with water flowing in the gutter. They got in.

Are you a journalist?

No.

Are you an American?

How can you tell?

I couldn't tell for sure, I simply guessed. A lot of Americans are here at the moment.

To be exact, I was born in China but am now an American citizen.

Then you are Chinese-American.

If you like, though there used to be a distinction between Chinese who lived temporarily in America and Chinese who emigrated. The latter were called Chinese-

Americans. It doesn't matter these days. Are you a journalist?

Yes, I am a journalist. I write articles on films.

Which paper?

At the moment I write for the *Journal*. What are you doing in this country?

I am not sure yet. I seem to sleep quite a lot. And I am also looking for an apartment with white walls and not too much furniture. Do you happen to know of one?

Yes. Some beautiful apartments are to be had in quarters overlooking parks and gardens. Only American millionaires can afford them.

While she listened to his talk she became aware that he was examining, in discreet sidelong glances, her hair under her rain hat, her suit, her legs and particularly her shoes. She noticed that he needed a shave and that his hair was cut and combed forward in the Edwardian fashion. He was tieless and his shirt was unbuttoned at the neck, a red and white checked shirt under a slightly limp dark blue suit. Seated as she was she could not see his shoes without having to bend forward. They were nearing the Circle.

I might take an apartment in this neighborhood. I looked at one yesterday. It has white walls and not too much furniture. Where do you live?

In the suburbs where it is absolutely quiet. I need silence for writing.

They approached the Avenue by a narrow side street but found the entrance blocked by huge red and white striped barricades on account of construction underway on the Avenue. The driver made a long detour and approached the Avenue from the opposite direction.

Let me give you my name in case you should want to reach me.

I'll know your name from reading your articles.

No, you'll forget.

He fumbled in his various pockets.

Let me put your name in my address book.

She passed a finger slowly along the alphabetical listing of her book. He took away the book.

You won't remember me under my name. I'll put it under T for taxi.

On the top margin of the T page he wrote his name, the name of his paper and telephone number in a tiny stiff script.

I shall be leaving for the sea to do a film but will be back probably Wednesday night.

When he returned the address book, she tore out a page from the back, wrote down her name and the name of her hotel.

I may not be there Wednesday since I am hoping to get that apartment near the Circle. I don't remember the exact address.

You might call the newspaper and leave word.

The driver stepped on his brakes to avoid a car which appeared without warning from a narrow side street just before they reached the Avenue. The taxi lurched to a stop. She fell forward from the seat and knocked her left knee against a metal fixture that stuck out in the separation between the two front seats.

Are you hurt?

She held her breath and did not answer him right away.

Did you tear your stocking?

She pressed her hand tightly against her knee where it hurt. When she uncovered it there was a bruised area where the skin had been torn off. The stocking surprisingly was intact.

You're hurt.

It's nothing.

The taxi drew up before the dentist's house. She was half an hour late for her appointment. They shook hands and she hurriedly opened the door on her side.

Good-bye. So very kind. Thank you.

As she made her way out of the car she remembered that she had not been able to close the back zipper of her skirt that morning. She hoped it did not show.

She took the 83 back to the hotel, had an early supper in a Chinese restaurant nearby and afterward sat through a film. When she entered her hotel room and turned on the light switch just inside the door, she saw at the far end of the room a vase containing pink and violet flowers packed tightly, the heads drooping. Someone had forgotten to add water in the vase.

The next day she telephoned but did not reach him so she left a message for him to call and the telephone number of her new apartment.

*N*gmah's birthday was always cele-
brated the last week in April. Several days before the
event, Dyadya telephoned them as usual from his office to
keep the plans a surprise for Ngmah. His terminating
admonishment before hanging up was to remind them
not to forget to send flowers.

But they did not need reminding. For so many years
every April he would remind them. That year, in order
of precedence, First Nancy sent a forsythia plant, Second
Katherine pink roses, Third Christine a basket of yellow

mums, Fourth Jane pink snapdragons four feet long, Sixth Michael white lilacs, how did he manage, and Seventh Jill pink, red, coral, wine geraniums, each color potted separately but packed together in a basket. Fifth James was out of the country and was not, therefore, represented.

Dyadya sat in his study and composed a letter. Dear James we are going to the Far East the beginning of September to return for the first time to that part of the world we left more than twenty years ago. Please join us there upon your leaving the Army. Seventh Jill who has never been in that part of the world will also come with us. Enclosed please find my check to cover expenses for your journey.

Ngmah sat in her study overlooking the park. She was was she the most beautiful of them all? She was altering the seams of a dress she intended to wear for her birthday dinner. She had spent more than twenty years letting out a fraction of an inch here, taking in a fraction there, lengthening and shortening. What a relief finally to go to the Far East to have clothes cut expertly and sewn to measure.

She made small even stitches, sewing neatly and rhythmically in time with her thoughts. All those lovely dresses that would be hers. The dress for James's wedding, what material should it be, brocade or lace, what woman among those eligible will he choose, help him choose.

The thread became too short to continue so she tied a knot and bit off the rest, pausing an instant to look out of her window before threading the needle. She saw a church steeple in the distance. Between the steeple and her window the park spread out in its lush spring newness. Shopping excursions to find the perfect material. Find a master tailor who knows the secret of perfect cutting, perfect shaping. Borders or no borders, button fasteners shaped like butterflies and hours and hours of fitting. The tailor kneels to pin and unpin. What length madam?

She hitched up the hem a fraction, looked into the mirror in front of her and two mirrors flanking her and another behind her. There release more. Perfect. She let the hem fall.

She threaded the needle and continued to stitch at the point where she had left off. Days, weeks, months, years, the pains of birth, absences, voyages, wars, losses, solitude, storms at sea, thirst and hunger, her Father dead, miles of silks newly dyed floating sullen and heavy in the waters of the canal, silks twisted and looped oozing dripping colors not yet fastened into the fabric from overnight soaking in the canal, silks unfurled and drying in the sun on the road by the edge of the canal.

They met at the apartment. Then in groups of threes and fours they went by taxi to the Chinese quarter to eat crabs and snails and carp tails and shrimps and spinach and bean curd and bitter melon, Ngmah's favorite, in honor of Ngmah's birthday. And happily the Spring holiday coincided with the occasion which brought home from school both Seventh Jill and Sixth Michael. Fifth

James who was stationed with the American Army in Germany was absent that year.

For the first time since they came to this country they were able to buy fresh lichees from street vendors in the Chinese quarter. Dyadya said Imagine the Chinese have brought the lichee tree to America and have planted it in American soil, in the South where the climate and soil are similar to certain southern regions where lichees flourish. He bought plastic packages of lichees for each of them and gave each vendor stationed at short intervals along the street a portion of his business.

They scattered wet peels and stones in the gutters as they strolled through the dusk crowded neon-lit streets of the Chinese quarter, silently following Dyadya who led the way and talked.

We celebrate Ngmah's birthday. We celebrate the arrival of lichees in America. Progress, change, growth, life. We celebrate our departure for the Far East. In a few months' time we will be joined there by James who is not with us tonight. Do you know the story of the empress and her caprice for lichees? She ruined the country. Couriers were posted along the highway built especially for the purpose of transporting the fruit. They sped on horseback in relays from the capital to the southern wilderness, returning north with full baskets to satisfy her thirst. Listen. She also loved the sound of tearing silk and spent mornings listening to the sound of tearing silk. Disastrous for the economy, silk being used as a measure of currency in those days.

They descended the garbage-strewn steps and entered a crowded sour-aired cavern lit by bluish fluorescent tubes in the ceiling.

Dyadya said What is essential is not the surrounding but the food.

When the drinks arrived Dyadya said Honor Ngmah. God has been with us and may he never leave us. He took us safely out of China. In the north the battle raged. Rails from the north converged where we were, bringing trainloads of the wounded and the retreating. I had orders to stay at my post to care for the wounded, most of whom were brought to me since I had the best X-ray equipment in the province, your grandfather's gift to me, and I stayed at my post during the retreat. At night we operated in the basement because of bombardments and Ngmah helped me after the nurses were told to go. Every night I wrote out my daily report as I was instructed. The night before the city fell, Ngmah and I disguised ourselves and we departed after the last remaining wounded had been evacuated in a bus provided by Miss Ironside the local American missionary. Ngmah and I made our way to headquarters as indicated in my written orders given to me at the beginning of hostilities. We made our way to various headquarters along the route of retreat. Each time we arrived headquarters had retreated further. In the southern capital, the end of the trek, I was not able to make my report, my superiors having fled, and we boarded the last boat to leave the city. Honor Ngmah who has never left my side. A courier arrived the other day. We drank tea in the living room. My hands were folded in my lap while I waited to hear his message.

Come back to us and help rebuild new China.

No, I have done my share. I am here to stay.

When the food arrived Dyadya said The lakes from which this particular algae grow and used to grow in prehistoric times were once part of the sea before they became landlocked. There is a fish which can be found only in these lakes, a fish related to the whale, smaller than the whale of the ocean but of the same species, which swim today in the China Sea. The stunted whales in the lakes feed upon this algae. During the Occupation the Japanese took samples of it to Japan and stocked their lakes with it. Today they export it to America in glass jars and we now have the pleasure of eating it in America.

He handed the first bowl of soup to Ngmah.

*S*he had not heard from him and wondered if he was still making his film by the sea or on a train returning to the city or had already returned and forgotten her since that first meeting. She undressed, took a bath and got into bed with several issues of the newspaper in which she had found his articles. When the telephone rang she was dozing. Would she meet him for dinner the next evening? Yes she would like to but what was he doing tonight? He wanted to see a film at nine-thirty. Would he like to come for a drink before the film? The apartment was terribly dirty and in disorder but she hoped he wouldn't mind. He wouldn't mind because he was terribly dirty too having been on the train all day. In that case would he please come right away, right away.

She took off her nightgown and put on a pair of white trousers and a pink jersey blouse. The doorbell rang just as she finished combing her hair. She threw the brush down and dashed to the door so happy to be alive.

She hung up his raincoat in the empty closet next to the bathroom then followed him into the two front rooms separated by wide sliding doors which she had kept open. One room contained a narrow uncovered bed with cushions which served as a sofa. Opposite the bed-sofa near the window was a plain long table, two chairs and a floor lamp. The adjoining bedroom contained a large bed and a small table with a lamp on top of it.

Do you like the apartment?

It's a bit bare.

I like it bare. Can I get you a drink?

She returned from the kitchen with two glasses of whiskey and found him lost in thought seated in one of the two chairs which faced each other across the width of the table.

What are you thinking of?

Nothing. I am listening to the silence and to the noise of your curtains brushing against each other by the window. Sounds like the sea.

She sat down on the other chair.

How did it go with your film? Is it finished? What is it about?

He didn't answer straight away, listening to the silence and the sea.

It's about two persons, a man and a woman, both of average middle class background. It is summer. The wife leaves town with their son to spend the summer in a house rented on the beach. The husband joins them only on weekends. I employed amateurs, people who never acted before. I gave them no dialogue but simply said Tonight is Saturday night. The husband has just arrived by train from the city. He is a physician as he is in real life. From the moment the husband enters the house by the sea on a Saturday night, husband and wife make their own dialogue. Then the son comes in. All this goes on for half an hour. They play their own lives.

May I get you another drink?

What time is it?

Nine.

Would you like to see the film? It's an old American one.

Is it far from here?

No, within walking distance.

I think not. I'm tired and don't feel much like getting dressed to go out. Perhaps another night.

He let the subject drop and sat still in his listening attitude, his head inclined slightly to one side. She left him and went into the kitchen to refill the glasses. When she returned he was examining a map which was lying on top of the typewriter on the table, a motoring map showing the major roads connecting the major cities of Europe. She handed him his glass.

Are you planning to travel?

I might go there.

She leaned across the table and pointed to a spot on the northern shore of the continent. My Father once studied there. Summers he used to take the ferry across to spend weekends in Denmark.

She folded up the map and placed it beside the typewriter.

Shouldn't you leave for your film now?

What time is it?

Nine-thirty.

Too late. The film has started.

I'm sorry. Was it important to see it?

It doesn't matter, it will come around again.

Would you like another drink?

No, not yet.

He got up and paced around the room.

I like to travel too. I have traveled through most of Europe and the Middle East. I've also been a short time in America, mainly in New York. I should like to go to the Far East but can't afford to do so.

Have you had dinner?

I'm not hungry.

If I were to cook a steak would you share it with me? And some string beans?

Yes, if you let me help you.

He followed her into the kitchen.

It's very hard to shop here. But then of course I don't

know where to go for things. I am used to another way of shopping, ordering enormous quantities by telephone once or twice a week. Here the few shops open in the summer close for four hours right in the middle of the day.

She took out a steak and a bag of string beans from the icebox and turned on the grill. He stood close behind her and watched in attentive silence as she washed the string beans and picked off the hard ends.

I'm going to take charge of the steak. Tell me when I should put it under the grill.

That's really very nice. Do you really want to help? Yes.

I should start the beans first, don't you think?

Yes, start the beans first but don't put too much water in the pot. The important thing is not to cook them too long in too much water.

You seem to know a lot about cooking.

Writers belong in the kitchen. Cooking is an essential part of their imaginative environment.

Oh. You can put in the steak now.

A bird plunged like dead weight ten stories from the roof. Two stories from the pavement, with a single flap of wings, it skimmed above the quivering treetops and took off in a sweeping spiral till it disappeared behind the rooftops.

We can eat now.

*A*t eighty-four she sat still and heavy as a stone at the end of the room in a high-backed chair beside which was set up a home movie screen. She stared with vacant watery eyes at all the bodies male and female young and old assembled before her and amah appeared at the door of the pantry with a stiffly iced white and pink cake brought to the country house the evening before from a German bakeshop on 86th Street by Dyadya on his way home from the office. And while the others sported in the garden, played hide-and-seek in the dense asparagus field, splashed in the pool, picked strawberries which grew among stalks of thin wild rye in the back field fronting the woods, or sent the tattered shuttlecock over the badminton net staked in the center of the lawn under the shade of two giant willow trees, trunks wide as an armspread, amah opened two packs of miniature candles, sorted out and counted eighty-four pink ones planted in eighty-four pink sugary holders and arranged them painstakingly in narrowing circles around the pink and mocha cream roses taking care not to obliterate the flowing thick script in chocolate cream Happy Birthday Grandmother, a phrase which the children were told to say when they entered the room and approached her to perform a neat obeisance, the little ones running up, pausing then shouting the phrase at her in English or Chinese whichever they were capable of, then running away immediately afterward so that she had barely time to acknowledge the greeting although occasionally she whispered machine gun the only word she could by now remember in English the sounds pleased her. The older ones lingered over her, bending to touch or clasp the hand which held the crumpled ball of handkerchief or the other which rested on the arm of the chair, and she would slowly turn her face toward the voice and the vacant indrawn expression would suddenly change into a deep lined smile if she remembered who you were when you said Grandmother I am so-and-so Happy Birthday and Many Happy Returns.

Dyadya summoned. Everyone came in from the garden to assemble in the living room, sitting on chairs, sofas, the carpeted floor. Dyadya said in Chinese We are together here today to honor our mother. Someone drew the blinds across all the windows of the room and Uncle Two switched on the projector and Grandfather's big grainy face flickered over the entire screen, intelligent assertive smiling broadly in love with life's hazardous enjoyments, his moving lips flickering head and shoulders refused to budge from the scene.

An offering to heaven First Nancy's face appeared on the lower left portion of the screen, an apparition superimposed on Grandfather's shoulder, unmoving against Grandfather's flickering silent animation, a forlorn face, round large eyes stared into nothing. Then her head began to turn with agonizing slowness, showing in profile hair cut straight at the ends, parted and combed to one side, clamped together by a large floppy bow tied at the back of the head. The velvet collar of her heavy chesterfield coat lay awkwardly on her narrow shoulders. First Nancy vanished and with her vanished Grandfather interrupted in the middle of a soundless anecdote recounted with emphatic shakes and nods of the head.

A house appeared, its clean fortress lines punctuated by black block windows possessed the screen. The front door opened. Ngmah in white stood in the doorway, wrapped in soft summer stuff, white panels swirling around her legs and ankles. She left the black rectangle and advanced haltingly toward the camera, giggled and screened her face with her hands. She wore her hair shingled and cut close to the head. All at once with short swaying steps, she fled back into the black rectangle and closed the door.

The camera retreated. The diminishing house gave way to a white cloudless sky and a gray lawn in the foreground. Black flooded the lower screen. Perhaps a flowerbed, a privet bush sent forth static messages in the watchful silence.

In front of the paved courtyard stood a house with a high porch. Aunt Two sat on the top step of the porch. Her hair was smoothed away from the face and coiled in a bun at the back. Fourth David stood on the step below, his waist embraced in his mother's arms, his head rested on her shoulder. He looked shyly into the camera. She looked at him then laid her forehead on his cheek.

He opened the door of the spare room and found her in bed.

What, still in bed? Why are you not dressed? The funeral is at eleven o'clock. It's already ten-thirty. We are leaving in a quarter of an hour.

I cannot go Dyadya.

What do you mean you cannot go? You have to go to your cousin David's funeral. We are all going.

I must be ill. I can't wake up. I can't move.

She lay unmoving and closed her eyes.

He looked at her in disbelief. Without further comment, he shut her door.

Third Edward arrived on the screen, his back to the camera. He climbed the porch, turned and sat down next to David still entwined in his mother's arms. He looked into the camera, smiled and placed his hand on his mother's shoulder. All vanished.

A wall encircled the courtyard. Aunt Two, First Albert, Second Violet, Third Edward, Fourth David and Tiny Grace linked hands forming a ring skipped and hopped round and round while the camera angled them from an upstairs window.

Lustrous sky, trembling river, a bargelike boat with ample decks docked by a black pier. Against the backdrop of the river three women hurried along the pier, faces half hidden by enormous fur collars wrapped and clutched tight around the neck by white-gloved hands. The wind whipped up their long ankle-length coats.

Three black figures, remote and legendary, outlined against the sheen of the sky. Pressed by a common errand, they hastened toward the barge. Aunt Three, then Aunt Two, and at last Ngmah walked up the short gangplank and stepped awkwardly onto the deck.

The barge churned upriver, passing precipices and gorges. Bare-chested coolies, gaunt shoulders weighed down by poles carrying sedan chairs came into view around the bend of the mountain track. Some paused to look into the camera before continuing on their slow-swinging way, bodies sagging under the load.

Beside the mountain track Grandfather sat astride a horse of weatherbeaten stone and interrupted his mad dash on horseback, elbows jerking and body heaving, to raise a hand in salute to the camera. What a lot of fun he's having. He turned toward the straggling line of porters and gestured like a commander on horseback encouraging the men upward.

In a clearing of bamboo thickets on a mountain peak Grandfather finished planting sticks of incense on all the burial mounds. Each time he lit a cluster of sticks they bowed low three times in front of the mound.

Light flooded the blank white screen. The loosened end of the tape beat against the whirring machine. Then the light went out.

Amah carried the cake lit by eighty-four candles into the dark, taking care not to trip or drop the cake. Everybody broke out into song Happy Birthday in English. Grandmother's eyes followed the path of the flickering lights, oblivious of the singing voices. Next to the last verse of the song where the birthday person is named, some sang out Dear Grandma or Dear Grandmother in English. A few voices sang out her title in Chinese.

Ngmah held up the cake to Grandmother. Blow blow voices cried in English and Chinese. She blew. Nothing happened, the flames flickered softly as before. Dyadya stepped up and blew, someone drew open the blinds and the afternoon sun poured into the room from the west windows through the trailing vines of spider plants on the sills behind Grandmother's chair. Pieces of cake were passed around. Amah cut and served.

Assembled in order of patrilinear precedence to eat Grandmother's birthday cake were Dyadya, Uncle Two and Aunt Three. Then the wives and Aunt Three's husband. After that came First Nancy Chen-Hua, Second Katherine Kwang-Hua, Third Christine Tswai-Hua, Fourth Jane Chuang-Hua belonging in name both to the male attribute and the female, Sixth Michael Chuang-Chu, Seventh Jill Lo-Hua who in the country went barefoot night and day in order to better control the pedals of the baby grand when practicing Telemann. Fifth James Chuang-Shin, the firstborn male soldiering for the American Army in Germany, was absent.

Partaking of that third generation but coming after due to the second position of Uncle Two in the previous generation were Second Violet Sing-Hua, First Albert Chuang-Liu soldiering for the American Army in Hawaii was absent, as was Fourth David Chuang-Wei dead from a virus the previous year, Third Edward Chuang-Pin and Fifth Grace Mei-Hua.

Partaking of the same generation but not belonging to the paternal line due to Aunt Three's change of name through marriage were First Lily Lai-Ling, Second Phoebe Yin-Ling, Third Matthew Pui-Ming, Fourth Paul Pui-Shing, and Fifth Cecilia Wei-Ling praising God in a convent in Indiana was absent that day.

Aunt Two fed a piece of cake to Grandmother. Grandmother chewed gravely, swallowed and gave forth a considerable burp. She spoke in a frail quavering voice. Out of my womb came these generations.

*R*ubber tubes inserted in various orifices man made and nature made and taped to her body she tore out and died alone before her eighty-fifth birthday early in the morning before the nurses came to take her temperature.

When she went to hospital for the operation, not performed by Dyadya this time, although she had wished it, not understanding why she could not have him do it as at that first operation after recalling him from university in Germany since she would not at that time have another doctor, she wept.

She hid the money Dyadya gave her since her arrival in America, bills of small denominations, her pocket money which she pasted singly and securely with adhesive tape on the back of the floor-length mirror nailed to the wall between two closet doors. And also pieces of jewelry still in her possession that she had not distributed in worth according to favor and disfavor among the women of the next generation, she hid in tiny silk bundles made out of leftover scraps of dressmakings. She lowered herself to the floor and crouched on her knees to stuff her bundles between rear crevices of radiator pipes. She made packets out of paper by folding three corners toward the center to form an envelope of calling card size into which she placed unset gems, separating kind and color, tucking the last corner neatly into the final pleat, in the Chinese way, and hid them in the toes of her quilted slippers with embroidered tops.

Toilet soaps provided another hiding place. Her long fingernails pried out holes into which she buried pearls accumulated on expeditions out of the walled compound into the city in company of household bodyguards. The holes she recovered by wetting and repasting soap slivers and smoothing over the rough spots with finger and water.

They dressed the corpse in pale gray silk, pulled white cotton stockings over the legs, encased the feet in plain black slippers with cotton quilted soles and laid her in a coffin of very solid bronze.

Dyadya, Uncle Two, Aunt Three stood in a row in front of Grandmother's coffin. Around her strong delicate fingers, perfect moons in tapering nails, was looped a brown wooden rosary. She worshiped Christ in her final years. Incense-filled ceremonies and the sound of bells brought her back to Buddha, fingers that had been capable of drilling holes through pearls and toting in the failing light two enormous cans of Libby's pine-apple juice, economy size, remembering at the last moment, trembling with the weight of her gift as she made her way hesitatingly down the steps of the porch, her good-bye to James already seated in the car ready to go, her son's son who was to leave for Germany to serve with the American Army the traditional welcoming and leave-taking gift of pineapple.

Dyadya turned to address his sister and brother in a loud voice. Our mother is dead, her children are left alone. Prescribed by custom as eldest son he led the dirge while the two others chanted along in polyphony.

Our mother is dead. Where will we find another? Her children are left alone in this world.

The others standing behind the first row kept silent, shuffled their feet and glanced at each other furtively. Uninformed, they suppressed a momentary bewilderment. Dyadya cleared his throat, composed himself and spoke in a normal voice.

Your children and children's children pay you our last respects.

The chorus drew out handkerchiefs and mopped their faces. Everyone in the room bowed three times to Grandmother. Someone from the funeral home approached and closed the lid of the coffin.

They filed out of the room past curtained windows of flowery chintz and chintz-upholstered armchairs, descended the narrow stairs carpeted in red and emerged into sharp wind and brilliant sunshine.

The hearse moved slowly along the potholed street, came to a deliberate and lengthy stop at the end of the road and then mounted a steep side road which forked into the broad expressway.

At the gates of the cemetery they left their cars and walked the rest of the way to the knoll where everyone assembled before the grave. A shiny green carpet of synthetic grass covered the fresh mound of excavated earth. They lowered the coffin into the trench while the priest intoned a prayer.

She stepped on the artificial grass, climbed to the top of the mound and peered into the trench. The coffin lay in a close-fitting trough of still damp concrete especially devised so that raising the coffin should not be too troublesome should it be decided one day to bring her back to China. They left the grave open till the next day, long enough for the concrete to harden before piling back the earth.

She hid from amah and wandered through the maze of courtyards and corridors to find the exact place where muttering voices and the hollow clatter of wood hitting wood issued from somewhere in the vast unfamiliar house. She found the glazed redwood door, reached up to pull down the handle and entered the fog-smoked room filled with square tables around which sat men holding cards and men stirring bamboo and ivory blocks, constructing with incredible speed the two-tiered four-sided mahjong wall.

She found the table where Grandfather sat with three other men. She had to stand on tiptoe to watch the game and rested her chin on the ledge of the table. In the center only one and one half wall remained untouched. Grandfather pushed back his chair and in one swift movement of both hands flung down his entire row of blocks face up—Pan!—to reveal the content and extent of his victory.

*A*fter clearing the table she piled dishes and pots into the sink and returned to the other room. She found him examining a page of financial statistics.

What are all these figures, what do they mean?

Each figure means something. Here, I'll show you. It starts at the left with the name of the company. Next to the company—165—is the approximate price it sells for today. These two figures 165 and 63 represent the highest price per share the stock reached during the year. Here, the lowest. After that the figure 133. Let's see, that's the percentage . . .

He yawned.

I'm sorry. Am I boring you?

No, no. It's very interesting. I'm sleepy.

I must have bored you but I like reading these figures. The meaning behind them can engage mind and imagination as much as words can without words' ambiguity. The content of each story is profit or loss, and the story can be enthralling depending on whether you have been committed or not.

She put aside the pamphlet.

How will you go home?

There's a bus that leaves at midnight.

It's already past midnight.

There're always taxis to be found in this neighborhood.

Would you like to stay here for the night?

Yes very much.

I am occasionally an insomniac.

In that case we can talk all night.

I have pills for that.

Americans take too many pills.

Perhaps. Though when I come to think of it we used to take quite a lot of pills in China. Daily rations of gray flat tablets for calcium slightly sweetened and chewable. Vitamin pills, injections of all kinds. There was a clinic at the end of the garden. Oh, are you falling asleep?

No I am quite awake.

Shall I run a tub for you?

Yes.

She went into the bathroom and turned on the taps after shutting the drain. While the water ran she took and swallowed a pill from a bottle in the medicine chest. Returning to the bedroom to fetch a towel from the cupboard, she found him standing bare-legged next to her bed. His trousers were crumpled in a heap on the floor. She avoided looking in his direction while he unbuttoned his shirt. She took a towel from the closet and hurried out of the room.

She entered the kitchen and turned on the light. The dishes and pots which had been piled into the sink earlier in the evening gave her something to do while he took his bath. As she washed she looked out from her kitchen window at the unlit windows across the dark airshaft. Working quickly and making as little noise as possible she had all the dishes rinsed and stacked on the drainboard by the time she heard water draining from the bathroom tub.

She turned away from the sink, turned off the kitchen light and went to the bedroom. She picked up his clothes from the floor and draped them on the back of one of the two chairs in the living room. Then she undressed, pulled away the covers of the bed and slipped between the sheets.

He had a towel wrapped around his stomach and he stood looking down at her inquiringly. She made a movement toward the side of the bed where he was standing and groped for the light switch somewhere along the lamp cord. He bent down and took the cord from her and turned out the light.

She woke up in the dark and wondered about the hour, remembered the silence before falling asleep after having been made love to. He had held her without moving for a long time. He had kissed her face it seemed for an equal length of time till he had kissed every part. She could not remember if he had come. She got out of bed without waking him and headed for the bathroom for the bottle of pills in the medicine cabinet.

She swallowed a pill and replaced the bottle on a bare shelf of the cabinet. Under the harsh beam of light hanging above the cabinet she saw her image, cut off at the waist, mirrored against the shadowed confines of dull porcelain walls. Her face appeared intolerably alien and unclaimed as the space and light around her.

She switched off the light and stepped softly into the dark in search of him. Dismissing the figure dimly asleep on one side of her bed, she ached for another's presence.

Why won't you wait till I come back?

I can't wait. Marry me now.

Her arms and fingers were sore and aching from pressing together the handles of a pair of garden shears. The thin willow trunk, straining under a final spasm, snapped raggedly in two. The top half spilled at his feet in a hush of tangled leaves and branches.

He looked at her perplexed and reproachful, then gently touched her arm that held the shears.

Come away with me then.

Haven't got time. Leaving in a few weeks.

She shook away his hand, stepped over the prostrate willow and went toward the climbing wisteria and the dwarf apple still standing in leafy splendor in wooden tubs by the two front corners of the terrace.

She needed something to look out on. The blinds were drawn down in the living room so she went out into the kitchen and sat perfectly still in the dim light made by a lighted window several stories above her in the airshaft outside her kitchen window.

*U*nder the light of the standing floor lamp amah sewed together a quilted cotton sole made up of layers of rough white cloth cut to shape. With her thimbled finger she pushed the needle slowly through the different layers till the point of the needle came out on the other side. Then she tugged and strained. The whole needle emerged and with it the double stranded thread looped through the eye. After that a tightening followed by another stitch which repeated the whole process. Stitch after stitch made circular patterns like age rings of tree trunks cut across in the middle. She sat motionless except for the movement made by her hand and arm plying the needle. She began to sing the fisherwoman's lament.

She stood at the end of the skiff skimming the surface of the water, her hands clutching a long pole which she drove in and hauled out of watery spaces covered in pools of mist and reed patches. Her husband drowned. Her sons drowned. She sang out the lines she remembered and hummed the tune softly to passages words she could not remember. Sometimes stopping to regain her breath she leaned motionless on her pole and listened to foxes howling on the shore.

Layers of cotton stitched together made a sanitary pad which soaked in a basin of bloody water on the white tiled floor between the white porcelain toilet stand and the white porcelain sink. Attached to each corner of the narrow cotton rectangle was a twisted cotton strap. A shallow basket of purple red lichees and yellow loquats stood beside the washbasin. Time for tea. They raised the toilet cover and seat and peeled their fruits, letting the peels fall into the bowl but tossing the stones into the basket.

On the way back to the house from the clinic, at an unfrequented turn of the cement garden walk pink under sunlight and bordered on either side by giant flowering cactus plants in full flower rooted in freshly raked soil, First Nancy stopped and said to the three others Now we will play. First Nancy played physician, Second Katherine nurse, Third Christine and Fourth

Jane raised their skirts, stepped out of their underwear and lay down on the hot cement with legs spread apart. First Nancy opened her metal box painted white with a red cross in the center and a handle on the side and searched inside for cotton and the bottle of mercurochrome which Second Katherine unscrewed. First Nancy generously painted the affected areas.

Amahs' voices called out for them. They ended the game and went indoors for supper.

When lights went out amah said There are many different kinds of ghosts who wander in the dark. It is important to distinguish one from another. You may happen to meet the water ghost and I will tell you how you can recognize such a creature. Her hair hangs over her entire face for she died by drowning. She cannot see, hear, smell or speak on account of mud caked in her eyes, nostrils, mouth, and ears. She walks with arms extended, groping her way toward you, her palms facing you. Slowly and stiffly as she advances she feels her way, feels your presence. She leaves trickles of water where she passes.

The ghost who died by hanging, her head is bent to one side depending on which side she fell at the moment the neck broke. Her feet do not touch ground but hover slightly above it. She has a swaying walk and her garments float around her. Whoever sees her, dies. Amah who used to be First Nancy's amah died two years ago. She was carrying First Nancy on her back. She mounted the circular stairwell to reach the room where all amahs sleep. As her foot touched the first step of the stairs a

cool draft swept by. She turned half around to look.
What she saw she died of a day later.

The ghost of one beheaded like that queen in the
film we saw walk up the scaffold a week ago Saturday
in town wanders headless in search of her head. Pity.
It's all shooting nowadays. If you get shot to death you
do not become a ghost. I am not sure about burning.

Amah got up from the edge of the bed and stepped
silently to the round marble-topped table white and
pink-veined by the window and switched on the lamp.
She dimmed the light by tucking sheets of newspaper
around the lamp shade. Then she returned to her place
on the edge of the bed.

Formerly the condemned were dressed in red on their
way to execution. Brides also wear red on their wedding
day just like criminals and like bride mouse in the
comic strip stepping out of her curtained palanquin to
be greeted at the entrance of her future home by
groom mouse and attendant mice. Her dress is red
though her veil and wreath are white. No, no not
Mickey Mouse not Minnie Mouse, this is the story of
Chinese mice. I'll let you sleep now.

The makeshift lampshade covering the lampshade
cast wide swatches of shadow on the walls.

Don't leave me amah.

Amah sat down on the edge of the bed and smoothed
out the apple green silk coverlet embroidered with
branches, birds and blossoms in varying shades of gray.

Once upon a time two persons were in love with one
another. One of them fell out of love and in love with

a third person. The one rejected threw acid on the face of the one who had left. The lover was kept bound in a chair in an empty room on the very top of a tower where there were no windows therefore no light. A flight of circular stairs wound from the base of the tower to the single door of that top room. One day the prisoner heard a noise coming from the base of the tower which sounded like a door opening. Screeches followed by cracks, a big bang, then silence. The prisoner heard chains dragging over stone. The sounds grew louder, echoes rising from the bottom of a well. No footsteps. Only the sound of heavy chains dragging slowly over stone steps. The prisoner suspected a connection between the dragging chains, the acid-torn face. Bound in that chair, fastened down in much the same way you have seen how in the films they execute criminals in America bound in a chair the lover began to struggle. The noise of chains approached the door. The door opened.

Amah fed her liquid medicine poured into a spoon from a bottle on the bedside table. She unrolled her pallet on the floor at the foot of the child's bed and covering herself neatly with a cotton quilt breathed evenly and fell asleep.

*H*e stood in the doorway of the
kitchen.

Can't you sleep?

No.

He picked up a glass from the drainboard and filled
it with tap water.

Are you hungry?

A little. What is there to eat?

He opened the door of the icebox. She noticed he

wore the same towel wrapped decorously around his waist.

I'll take another pill.

No. Eat something instead.

I'll make some soup.

He shut the icebox door, plunging them again in darkness. She went into the hall and turned on the light there so that she could see in the kitchen. He sat down on the chair in the corner where she had been sitting. She opened the cupboard just above his head and took out a can of soup which she opened and emptied into a pan.

Would you give me the milk?

He opened the icebox, reached in for the bottle which he handed her. She poured some milk into the pan, lowered the flame, and stirred. She added more milk.

Don't put in too much milk. I'm not American.

They ate the soup without talking or looking at each other.

Any bread?

She got up and took out a package of water biscuits from the cupboard overhead.

No bread in this house. We don't eat bread.

And in the spring bloated corpses flowed in the current of the yellow river, bobbing among torn roots and bits of watermelon rinds gnawed to the skin flowed under the bridge connecting their land to that of the local military commander who cultivated sugarcane scientifically in the Japanese way. By the riverbank under the shadow of the wooden bridge they dug in the shallow water for that sweet red-skinned ling shaped like tightly closed lips. Then they dashed across the bridge to the other bank and into the waving cane fields. Their amahs hacked away at the slenderest stalks of cane on the edge of the planting, choosing the reddest, therefore most tender and full of juice inside sweet to chew and suck on. They sat in the field of canes their backs to the bridge. In the distance they saw the gray city walls saw-toothed against argentine skies.

*T*he barbarian stood outside the barred gates of the wall. After fruitless years of patient search, with gnawing heart, she found a weakness along the immense wall encircling the garden, found, followed, married Fifth James and entered the garden at dusk.

Who is she they asked upon receiving James's letter which arrived over a quiet weekend with news that he would first marry then travel before coming home. His letter said they had met her once when they came up to the university for a one-day visit.

Dyadya spent the afternoon writing drafts but could not unknot his paralysis to translate and articulate his thoughts in words particularly as his thoughts were in Chinese while the words by necessity had to be in English. He summoned Second Katherine and Fourth Jane who arrived in the evening and together they composed a letter, a nice compromise between Chinese thought and English expression, to ask James to put off the marriage till he came home as he had been absent for more than two years.

Ngmah said I will go and see for myself what it is all about. Second Katherine and Fourth Jane, sweating in the heat of early summer, added that bit to the composition but Father said after the letter had been dropped down the mail chute by the back door No Ngmah had never left his side the letter will do and James will return.

James's second letter postmarked from Greece stated that they had already left on their travels and would be married shortly once they could establish residence requirements and obtain a permit. They traveled for nine months in Europe and the Middle East and by frugal spending managed to stretch their resources, James's army pay and the check Dyadya had made out to James for his trip to the Far East.

In Istanbul they stayed a fortnight to wait for the necessary papers. Dyadya, who had tried unsuccessfully to reach James while he was traveling with the barbarian, finally received news of the marriage in the form of a letter written in pencil on lined yellow foolscap, addressed to Dear Father and Mother. She was looking forward to meeting them again, regretted they opposed the marriage. She and James were having a wonderful time very happy and hoped that eventually they would be reconciled and accept her and be happy too. There were passages describing places she and James passed through. Nothing exotic phased them. In a hotel in Istanbul's native quarter they had been kept awake all night by bedbugs in their mattress.

She walked behind James through the gate of the tall white fence separating the kitchen lawn from the main garden, waved in by smell of lilacs in full bloom clustered along the length of the fence, purple and white still visible in the fading light. Ngmah turned on the light by the semicircular sofa in the living room where Dyadya sat alone the half hour before their arrival. James entered and sat a few feet away from Dyadya on the same sofa and the barbarian joined James at the edge end.

Dyadya said James then lapsed into silence. Ngmah entered from the kitchen with a tray of cups and saucers and a pot of tea. After pouring and placing three cups of tea on the round scallop-edged acacia table encrusted with ivory roofs, petals of mother-of-pearl and ebony branches, she moved away from the glow of the lamp and sat in an armchair by the fireplace.

Dyadya addressed James in English.

Did you have a good trip?

Yes we had a very good trip.

She shuffled her feet in desultory and nervous movements, scuffing up the carpet. She picked up the drawstring pouch lying in her lap and placed it by her feet. Small hands with spare, birdlike fingers twisted and tugged at the voluminous folds of her skirt that barely concealed the body's angularities. Now and then she raised a hand to finger a loose curl escaped from the haze of fine wavy hair which glowed an orange aureole against the lamplight. She wore it combed back and fastened in a tight bulging knot held together by a hammered copper clip at the back of the head.

Dyadya broke the silence.

We have been waiting for you. It would have been better if you had waited. You should have waited.

We wanted very much to get married. We wanted to travel and it seemed to us a good opportunity since we were abroad to do both rather than come back and wait. We are sorry if you do not think we did the right thing. Besides she has a crowd of relatives whom she did not want at the wedding and that was why we decided to do what we thought was the sensible thing.

Why do you say we? I am addressing you as my son.

She got up from the edge end of the sofa, picked up her drawstring pouch and moved toward Ngmah in the shadows.

Mother would you like to see our marriage certificate? She handed Ngmah a blue certificate about the size of a postcard folded in the middle. Pasted and stapled on to it was a photograph of James, a photograph of the girl both looking unkempt and fierce as if they were related, on either side of the crease.

Ngmah glanced at the certificate, placed it without a word on the broad arm of her chair and folded her hands in her lap. The girl turned to the fireplace and tentatively reached out to touch the two objects lying on the black stone mantelpiece. An elephant tusk intricately carved in the shape of a boat with pleasure-seekers leaning languid over open windows that opened and closed on silver hinges. Rigid banners flew topmast at bow and stern. Beside the boat lay a dark carved wood handle curved and rounded out at either end. Each end cushioned a carved jade disk, symbol of authority.

She moved across the room, swinging her pouch, and stopped in front of the three-paneled coromandel screen upon which were transfixed ladies and attendants frozen in gesture and pose under porticos and in courtyards inclining over arched bridges admiring weeping willows. She continued her way to the open door from which she had first entered and peered into the dark garden drowned in smell of lilac and hum of crickets. She returned to Ngmah.

Now that I am James's wife and a member of the family I hope we will get along. I am so eager to know all about you. I hope you will tell me all about yourself and teach me how to cook your way. James loves your food and so shall I when I learn how to tell the real from the fake. I know it will please James. I'm so eager to know everything because I want to be one of you.

She returned to her place on the edge of the sofa, put her arm around James's shoulder and caressed the back of his neck. Suddenly she leaned forward turning to Dyadya and in a hushed voice slowly said Father we are sorry we did not come home for the wedding but in all fairness I am certain we can work out an arrangement. I will share him with you fair and square.

Dyadya roared, raised his clenched fist in the air to bring it smashing down on his own knee.

Share? Share my son? James is my son he belongs to me. He is my firstborn son of my flesh and blood and through him are my other sons born as I am my father's son and he the son of my grandfather. His pain my pain, his defeats my defeats, his success my success, his love my love, his blood my blood, his right my right, his straightness mine. And until I die defects and nobility, rights and wrongs, strength and weakness, cruelty and kindness, all that is mine, is in me, comes of me and returns to me. You did not ask my permission to take what is mine. I never gave it. You married in the dark not in the light. You are giving me permission to share my son with you! I never gave you permission to take my son. What is mine unless I give it must be asked of me. My daughters of my flesh and blood I gave away. I gave permission to the men who asked me permission. Each one of them faced me in the light and asked my permission.

The pallbearers stood in the shadows twelve abreast between the double portals of the church and the doors of the inner chapel twenty years older than when some of them as ushers stood in the same receiving shadows dressed identically save for the blue cornflowers in buttonholes to bow in family and friends invited to First Nancy's wedding many hot summers ago. Gordon and Percy and Chia-Tseng who came from the Argentines, Chia-Wei, Consul Chia-Po, former Chief Magistrate Li, former Bank of China Hsi, Professor of

Philosophy Lo, tennis champion of Tsinghua, class of 1935, cousins First Albert and Third Edward and World Health Organization Tang and Peter Too. Dyadya's flower-blanketed coffin was placed in the center of the aisle in front of the altar where two candles dimly flickered.

Bride and groom held stage and Dyadya who stood slightly away from the center as required by American custom stepped up as he had been told to do when the minister said Who will give away this woman? And he mopped his brow and said I will.

Dyadya did not give her away but kept his First and all his rest in self-raging love and self-sweet bondage.

A line of black cars hired for the occasion waited at the curb, the gray hearse at the head of the line waited for the load. Mourners milled on the steps. Opposite the church on a cement island in the middle of the roadway three women clothed in black stood starkly outlined against the river empty of traffic this Sunday morning. Their veils fluttered in the stiff wind blowing across a piercing blue sky.

Where is First Nancy Dyadya called herding the children one by one down the steps into the Underground at the end of the day's outing. He turned his face and squinted in the glare of the setting sun. Nancy came forward and hurried down the steps to join the others in the dark enclosure. One by one the children went through the turnstiles First Nancy coming last.

Nancy you are my firstborn and you are to lead

Dyadya said. James you are my firstborn son and you are to lead.

They returned to their hotel facing Kensington Gardens in the raw gloom of a November evening. Once in their rooms Dyadya emptied the brown paper bag filled with fresh spinach which he had bought at the exit of the Underground. He washed the plant's pink roots and all in the bathroom sink, careful to pick out of the water the spoiled from the good, laying the dripping leaves on a clean white bath towel spread out on the bottom of the bathtub. He crouched on the carpet in front of the alcohol burner beside the radiator in the living room. He emptied two cans of chicken broth into the pot heated by a noiseless licking blue flame. When the liquid came to a boil and steam began to rise, he broke two eggs into the soup and immediately stirred. Then into the soup he added spinach which First Nancy carried out of the bathroom in a white hotel towel.

The children crouching around him stared at the spinach wilting in bubbling liquid, breathed in waves of familiar odors bringing to memory meals eaten in another place.

After they had looked at each other's beggar's repositories and admired and coveted Second Katherine's newest acquisition to her repository, a real walnut shell, the seam in the center intact, two sides which opened on hinges to show a tiny marionette on her toes, First Nancy said Close your boxes. Now we must pray.

Lisa the Austrian would be coming any minute still powdered and made up and scented at the end of her day off to put out the light. Blond Scots amah had put the boys to bed. Katie the Irish cook with mouse-colored hair had banked the fire in the iron stove and turned out the lights in the kitchen.

They climbed up First Nancy's bed. They knelt on the quilt and made a sign of the cross as the sisters had taught them to do at the last school they attended. First Nancy led and said out loud Our Father Who art in Heaven and they followed. Amen concluded, First Nancy opened the tattered varnish-cracked blue hymn book which she had taken from the last school and started to sing All things bright and beautiful All creatures great and small. They bent toward the open book in her hand unable to read the words but remembering a few by rote though not knowing yet the meaning hummed the notes to words they did not know except for First Nancy who more advanced knew how to read the new language and sang out clearly all the words of all seven stanzas of the song.

*H*e said he would call her in a day or two when he would come to town. But she did not hear from him so on the fourth day after his first visit she telephoned and left word at his office that she had called.

A day later she wrote him a note to his office. In the note she asked him to come the following Saturday and that she would roast a chicken for dinner. Late Friday evening when she had received no response, she went to bed early and woke up sometime in the morning just before daybreak. Not able to sink back into sleep she got out of bed, overwhelmed by an urge to cook.

As usual when it was dark outside she made faint light in the kitchen by turning on the light in the hall and leaving the door open between the two rooms. She took her time preparing an elaborate meal for a guest uncertain to appear. She rinsed the chicken under hot running water and placed it on the drainboard. Then she sliced stalks of celery crosswise, also an onion, and then lit the flame under a frying pan into which she put a large pat of butter. While the onion and celery browned in sizzling butter she added the gizzard and the liver, both thinly sliced. She stirred, placed a lid over the pan and turned the flame very low.

With her hand she crushed open fresh walnuts, two at a time, and picked out the damp fragments of meat. After she had accumulated a cupful, she added that to the pan.

She filled a deep pot with water into which she emptied a package of wild rice, lit another burner and placed the pot on top of it. Several times she uncovered the frying pan to give the contents a thorough stir either to even out the cooking or to add pinches of bay, thyme, oregano, salt and pepper.

She opened the window of the living room and leaned out over the railing. The curtains billowed by the damp wind blowing through the silent and deserted street made noises like the sea. She heard a scream.

A drunk staggered between parked cars, pausing for support at every car along the tree-lined pavement. All at once he embraced a nearby tree and clasped it to his chest. An instant later he began to vomit, emitting a sharp scream at each new convulsion of body which preceded a surge of vomit. Finally he fell still and resting inert, braced by the tree, his arms hung slack at his sides. Had he fallen asleep she wondered or had he died at the last upheaval he was so still. Smells from the kitchen brought her away from the window. She returned to the kitchen and saw that the rice had begun to boil. She stirred vigorously to unstick some grains which were clinging to the bottom of the pot.

She returned to the window and leaned out on tiptoe over the railing but could not immediately find her drunk. Then further down the street she saw him fumbling at the door of a car. He managed to open a rear door and climbed in like an animal burrowing into the entrance of a hole.

In the kitchen she added the drained rice to the mixture that was frying in the pan. With a spoon she stuffed the hot filling into the hollow of the chicken, sewed and placed it in the oven. She set the temperature at precisely midpoint between one-fifty and two hundred, went back to bed and fell into a deep sleep.

Light came through her bedroom shutters when she woke up with a rush of longing. How to fill the hours till his coming or not coming. And if he were to come how to fill the hours, minutes, seconds during his presence. She would have to go to the bank and after that to the hairdresser. Before leaving the house she turned off the oven.

Between the bank and hairdresser's she searched for him among the passersby. She stopped to buy a newspaper at a kiosk a few yards from the entrance of his office building, missing a heartbeat as she paid the vendor so hopeful of finding him right behind her when she turned around clutching his newspaper. At a pedestrian crossing she glanced furtively at the homebound crowd but she did not find him. Arriving at her apartment she dropped her keys in her fumbling haste to open the door. She had heard a distant ringing of a telephone.

She closed the door from the inside and while leaning against it sang a song to change the pace. Eternal Father strong to save Whose arm doth bind the restless waves Who bids the mighty ocean deep Its own appointed limits keep Oh hear us when we cry to Thee For those in peril on the sea. She ate two hard-boiled eggs, took a bath and went to bed.

It was dark when she woke. Enormous dark watery ribbons floated on the wall. She lay without moving so as not to give an indication of her presence. Amah rose from the foot of the bed her hair almost covering her face.

Can't you sleep?

She moved to the head of the bed.

Death by bamboo. For certain offenses the prisoner was bound to stakes in the ground under which bamboo seedlings had been freshly planted. The prisoner was left a lingering death while young sprouts grew through flesh. Death by flaying. Bit by bit they cut away the skin till the entire body became one skinless lump of bleeding flesh. This is the traitor's death. The most dreadful of all is punishment for matricide or patricide. The criminal is hacked into one hundred pieces. Starting out with the extremities the executioner chops off toes and fingers, ears and nose. Gradually he works his way toward the trunk of the body.

Amah fed her a spoonful of medicine, returned to the pallet at the foot of the bed and went to sleep.

The telephone rang.

Is the chicken in the oven?

Who is it?

Did I wake you up?

I didn't think you were coming.

Well then, go back to sleep. I can come another time.

No. Come now.

She quickly hung up the receiver fearful he might say no.

She apologized for not having finished dressing before he came.

You know, I left several messages which you did not answer. I really did not know whether you would come or not.

I don't like to telephone.

Why?

One never asks why.

Oh.

Talking to you on the telephone can be rather exasperating. You either don't understand or you're half asleep. As of today I shall not telephone you any more.

I'm not asleep all the time.

He followed her to the bedroom and watched as she sat on the edge of the bed to put on stockings. She got up and lifted the hem of her slip to hook her stockings to the garters.

Are you getting dressed to go to the opera tonight?

I am getting dressed because you are dressed.

She concentrated on buttoning the double row of buttons in the front of her pink dress, then opened the closet door to see herself mirrored on the inner side of the door. She brushed her hair forward. When her hair covered her entire face she felt and grasped a clump of hair from the crown. Holding it away from her head she teased it by brushing it downward. This she continued to do methodically, clump by clump, all the while pretending not to notice him although she could see vaguely through the thinning curtain of her hair his figure leaning against the doorway. He had a thoughtful expression on his face and he puffed a cigarette.

When her face finally emerged free from her hair, he shook his head slowly and in disbelief as if she had done something quite peculiar.

He hardly ate the chicken she put on his plate. While she was clearing away the dishes from the kitchen table he started to gnaw the forefinger of his left hand. She pulled his hand away from his mouth.

What's the matter?

He did not reply but pressed his teeth harder against the finger.

I have a fresh pineapple for dessert.

No thank you madam.

Would you like coffee?

No madam.

He pushed back his chair, got up, left the kitchen and returned an instant later smoking a cigarette.

After the dishes had been washed and rinsed and left to dry, she looked at him and saw that he was once more gnawing his finger. She dried her hands on her apron, leaned across the table and pulled his hand away from his mouth.

What's the matter?

The Chinese are a terrible people. They have infinite patience, they know how to wait. They are able to out-wait anyone in the world.

What's on your mind? I am very impatient. You must be joking.

No madam.

You are formal tonight. Are you angry?

No.

He got up and she followed him into the bedroom where he stretched out on the bed. She sat facing him at the foot of the bed.

Madam. Madam is used for erotic effect in dramatic conversation. Occurring at the climax of an avowal or denial, it is the admission of passion.

Give me an example.

He recited two unconnected lines of verse which terminated in the word madam. He sat up, put his feet on the ground and again recited the same lines. Both times declaiming the word madam, he stamped a heel into the carpet. Then he fell back on the bed.

She bent down and kissed him.

Will you stay the night?

Yes.

And cut my hair?

Yes.

She undressed and brought him a towel and a pair of scissors from the cupboard. He knelt on the floor before her body stretched out on the bed.

Can you see? Do you need more light?

No.

He took his time cutting. Starting from the top he combed the hair upward, cutting those hairs that stood up between the spaces of the teeth. As he continued downward, combing and cutting, he protected her sex by pressing his fingers softly over it. On the ridge rising between the inner part of her legs and her sex sheltered by his fingers, he snipped off the hair rapidly without aid of comb, cutting not too close to the skin because of the hair which curled and tangled there.

He picked up the loose end of the towel under her body and with it brushed off the hairs. Then he raised her hips to draw away the towel which he took compactly folded into the bathroom. He returned with another towel which he had soaked in very hot water, then wrung out, and placed it folded and steaming between her thighs. He turned out the light, lifted her and placed her between the sheets.

With a clang amah pulled out the stopper from the hole in the sink. Water rushed down the pipes in choking gurgles. Amah finished washing Third Christine. Her turn next.

Amah was taught to be clean and with a vengeance she kept her charges clean. Her nails bore relentlessly through the hair, tore sickeningly against the tense scalp. She felt her face pushed lower into the hole of the basin. Her hands groped and found the sides of the basin to which she clung for support. Rivulets of soap blinded her eyes, streamed down her face, into her ears, her nose and down her neck. Stiff and unbreathing she thought she could stand it no longer but suddenly she felt water being poured by the cupfuls on her head, the noise of the tumbler catching the water from the tap, and breathing deep with relief heard her wet hair squeak from cleanliness through amah's fingers.

She wrenched her head free from the weight of his shoulder in order to take in deep gulps of air. Mute roars raced through caverns of her head. Clasping his body tightly, she tensed her hip muscles and in a final effort rose and met him.

*D*yadya sat in the violet armchair next to the German radio phonograph of bleached blond ash in the music corner at the end of the living room. Seated there one could see almost the entire entrance hall through the wide connecting door always left open to better keep track of comings and goings at the front door except during piano lessons and Chinese lessons and French lessons before the girls started going away to college. And the front door was kept unlocked up to the night when burglars looted the unoccupied apartment of hi-fi equipment, carpets, cameras, silver, and jewelry scattered in Ngmah's drawers and smashed Seventh Jill's pink supersized piggy bank loaded with quarters of thirteen years' collection the summer James came home.

The view from the armchair also included the long corridor giving on to all the bedrooms. It began at one end of the entrance hall and ended at the last room which belonged to Dyadya. On another side of the living room a pair of double doors, two folding panels on each side, kept open a part of the dining room in view and the door to the pantry.

Dyadya's other armchair in his room at the end of the corridor was placed in line with the length of the corridor. It had a reclining back and a movable foot rest which could be raised and lowered according to the inclination of the sitter, and embraced a view of the corridor, the entrance hall, all the way to the music corner of the living room and the violet armchair.

Unless he was in bed or in the kitchen or not at home, he was to be found usually seated in either armchair reading, meditating or dozing, surrounded by neat piles of magazines, newspapers and financial reports. Sometimes he would go into the small study next to his bedroom if he had letters to write or figures to calculate on an electric adding machine which rested on the white formica desk ledge. Built into the wall, it had drawers on either side in which he kept documents and papers such as certificates of medical studies completed in China, Germany and America, assorted travel documents, and official papers, military decrees in Chinese, yellowed postcard mementoes of a week in Torquay with Mr. and Mrs. Stiff, watches purchased in Geneva, cameras, old sturdy Parker fountain pens, stamps and paper clips, a rubber doll from the Folies Bergères, a thank-you note in a thin box of handkerchiefs presented to him by a woman whose handbag he had found in the subway and returned, his Zeiss microscope in the square black box, surgical instruments hurriedly picked from the glass-doored cabinets of his clinic and packed into his black physician's bag in the dark, leaving the rest to the Japanese who took the city in the morning, a commemorative medal from the World's Fair of 1939, collected on the occasion of his first visit alone to America, children's school bills, letters from those who entered and left his life, people from whom he received and to whom he gave he could not part with.

Above the ledge shelves of books wall-to-wall rose up to the ceiling. Hardbacked books mostly on men of action he read from cover to cover, in some he had pasted reviews neatly clipped from newspapers, and how-to books on finance, accounting and gardening. On the very top shelf beyond normal reach, he had placed his collection of thick, somber volumes on medicine. On the bottom shelf just above the adding machine were tattered copies of Mengtse, Kungtse and works of minor Chinese philosophers and several copies of the *Tao Te Ching* translated into English by a literary friend.

The *Tao* he read in English, together with the Chinese text, covering both texts with marginal annotations in English and Chinese during the first year after James's marriage.

She came back from her wanderings earlier than usual though it was after supper time but still light out-doors. She entered the front door and found the house almost dark. No lights were on in any of the rooms. Thinking herself alone she made for the music corner in the living room to put a record on the phonograph but stepped back in alarm when all at once she saw him enveloped in the armchair, his eyes open and staring at her. In the failing light from the window she had noticed only the silhouette of the chair.

I didn't think anyone was home.

They've gone to see a film. You are early tonight for a change.

Yes.

You've been drinking.

I drank a glass of beer.

You drink too much. You should not drink too much. It affects the liver. Some day you'll end up with cirrho-sis of the liver. It's bad for your health. Have you had dinner? I brought back some dumplings from a res-taurant on my way home. They are in a box in the kitchen.

Thank you Dyadya. Can I get you anything?

He sat unmoving in his chair without answering her immediately.

Perhaps a glass of tea. Yes bring me a glass of tea.

She went through the double folding doors into the dining room and entered the pantry. In the kitchen she picked up the kettle on the stove, poured out the tepid water within, refilled it with fresh from the tap and set it back on the burner. From the window of the kitchen she looked at the violet light outside and the gradual lighting up of windows of buildings she saw him seated unmoving and silent in his violet chair. The kettle whistled, she poured boiling water over leaves in the tall glass.

She brought him the glass of tea on a plate. He took it, posing plate and glass on the arm of his chair and waited for swirling leaves to settle down at the bottom of the glass.

She wanted to leave the room, afraid he might raise the subject.

May I bring you anything else Dyadya?

When are you leaving?

She defended herself by replying in English.

Tomorrow Father.

I have been clearing out the spare room. I threw out a lot of empty cartons and took out Michael's bicycle and had it moved to the basement. There is much more space now. Much more comfortable for you. It doesn't look like a storage room now.

I've already signed the lease Father. I have bought a bed, a table and several chairs.

You must not drink too much.

Yes Father.

Will you know how to take care of yourself? Take care of your eyesight and read only under good light conditions. Do you have enough money? Ask me if you do not have enough.

I have enough. Thank you Father.

He looked away from her toward the radio phonograph. Interpreting that as sign of dismissal she left the room though hesitantly as if expecting him to call her back which he did not do.

She turned on the light at the head of the corridor and entered the spare room next to his. Her own room she had turned over to Second Katherine who after a three-year absence, came home and having made a try at living in it for a few weeks, found it inconvenient on account of the baby. Ngmah's empty cartons had been cleared away and the bicycle was gone. The folding card tables were still stacked against the wall next to the headboard of the bed, but the ironing board had been folded together and set into a corner of the room.

She packed slowly, unhooking the dresses from the hangers and laying them flat on top of each other on the bed. She folded the dresses one by one and placed them in the suitcase lying open on the floor beside the bed. She had packed and unpacked so often, always leaving from and returning to the same point, she knew the gestures by heart, could repeat them in sleep.

She heard footsteps in the corridor and momentarily paused in the folding of a garment. She stepped outside into the corridor but found it empty. Not a sound in the entire apartment dark except for the light in the corridor and from the spare room. She ran down the corridor into the dim entrance hall and stopped at the threshold of the living room.

Dyadya?

There was no answer. She pressed on the light switch by the door. He was bending over the violet armchair his back toward her. She went up to him.

What's the matter Dyadya?

He held a crumpled handkerchief with which he dabbed in slow motion an area of the seat cushion.

I spilled the tea. I must have fallen asleep.

He continued to dab the handkerchief against the cushion, pressing attentively and gently as if he were cleaning a wound. She cried soundlessly, tears streaming down her face.

Let me do it Dyadya.

He seemed not to have heard. He pulled up the seat cushion and groped between the crevices of the chair. He came up with a handful of soggy tea leaves which he carefully placed on the handkerchief he held in his other hand.

She touched his hand and at the same time took the handkerchief from him.

Let me do it Dyadya.

He stood by and watched while she picked out the last leaves from the crevice and replaced the seat cushion. He reached out for her hand, held, and kissed it.

He once made the three-hour drive from the city and stopped the car in front of the steps of her dormitory in his old Cadillac newly painted blue. He did not exchange the old for a new, that year being a recession year but all the same for the sake of change he had had the old one painted.

Do you like the color? Yes but she had not asked him to stay to tea. She had a lot of papers to write, a lot of reading to do over the weekend. As a matter of fact she was about to hurry over to the library just when he arrived if only she had known he was coming she would have prepared . . .

He unlocked the trunk of his car, raised the lid and pulled out the new portable Royal typewriter. He placed it on the bottom of the pink soapstone steps and returned to the car. Seventh Jill who had remained in the car throughout the exchange leaned out of the window and said nothing.

Good-bye take care of yourself and he got back into the car and drove all the way back to the city. She carried the typewriter up the steps of the dormitory, went into the dining room to finish her cup of coffee before going off to the library.

*A*t the head of the corridor she whispered to Second Katherine. Hearing her name she slowly turned away from the wall midway up the corridor against which she was leaning. They met and embraced in the wide passage brilliantly lit from the ceiling and smelling of antiseptic.

Have you just arrived?

Straight from the airport. Where is he?

I can't find him.

What do you mean?

They must have moved him into another room since the hemorrhage started. He isn't in the room where we last left him.

He must be somewhere nearby.

Second Katherine nodded toward the partially open doorway near which she had been leaning earlier.

He used to be in that room.

The doctors are in there talking. But he is not there. I don't understand what they are saying. They are discussing the case. We shouldn't interrupt them.

Side by side they made a tour of the U-shaped corridor, peering into every open room. They found him in a room right next to the one from which came the low voices of the doctors. His head and shoulders were propped up by two pillows. The blinds across the wide windows were pulled all the way up. He faced the lights of the city glittering softly in the night. A metal tube, an inch in diameter, was inserted in his throat. It stuck up like a periscope and prevented him from closing his mouth. Large glass bottles of thick liquids hooked on chrome rods flanked either side of his bed fed him nutrition through rubber tubes inserted in his skin and taped rigidly to his bare arms by white adhesive strips.

He turned his head slowly toward the doorway, the head moving upon the axis of the periscope, eyes glazed with pain, not seeing at first but hearing steps at the doorway.

She stepped up to the bed barred on each side by metal bars. Groping under the sheet she found his hand which he attempted to raise. She crouched and pressed her face between the bars and kissed his hand.

His lips moved around the barrel of the tube. Only hoarse windy noises came from his throat. He would not give up the attempt till she had made out the words.

When come back?

He moved his hand. Not understanding she released her hold until she realized by his fumbling that he was searching for hers. She gave him her hand which he raised to his mouth, having forgotten for an instant the impediment planted there. He placed her hand against his cheek and kept it there.

Second Katherine stepped forward to the other side of the bed and clung to his other hand.

All at once his body tensed, an anxious expression came over his face. He shifted his legs restlessly under the sheets, raised both tube attached arms and made quick spirited gestures in the air just above his head. They looked at him bewildered and helpless. He patted his head. When they understood finally that he wanted to comb his hair, his agitation subsided. She brought out a comb from her bag and put it in his hand. He combed his hair slowly. The rubber tubes quivered with each slow motion of the arm.

By the entrance of his office they waited for the elevator to take them down.

We shall have a good lunch. Where shall we go today for a good lunch?

Wherever you want to go Dyadya.

He started to pick at something on her coat near the collar.

What is it?

A piece of thread which does not belong.

By the front door of the apartment they waited for the elevator to bring them down. Suddenly he leaned over and with his bare hand brushed vigorously the hem of First Nancy's coat.

What is it?

It looks like a smudge of powder or ashes which does not belong.

He looked around and examined each of his own, found a dangling hairpin about to fall off Second Katherine's hair, which he undid from the hair and handed to Katherine, noticed Third Christine's outmoded coat, threadbare around the edges and made a mental note to take her shopping, a speck of dirt clinging to Fourth Jane's cheek which he brushed off with his hand, and patted Ngmah's arm in satisfaction for not having found anything askew on her. Seventh Jill home from school wore her waist-length hair in a single thick braid which hung behind her back. He touched her braid.

It is very well done. We shall have a good dinner tonight in celebration of your return home.

When he finished combing his hair he glanced at Second Katherine and Fourth Jane and waited for their approval. Both nodded, smiled and reclasped his hands.

A doctor bent over him.

How are you, how do you feel?

Hoarse noises coming from his throat finally took shape.

My Fourth . . . you have not met . . . today returned abroad.

And content with having done the proper thing in effecting the introduction, he sighed and settled back on the pillows.

*T*o stop the hemorrhage they cut him open for the second time in three days and worked on him from eight in the morning until three in the afternoon after which they wheeled him into a room and shut the door. There was no hope the doctor said. He was alive but would not last the night.

At five in the afternoon his heart stopped beating. They cut him open for the third time and brought back the beat by massaging his heart. The doctor said he would not last the evening. They cut a slit in his throat into which they inserted a machine so that he could breathe his last.

Ngmah sat erect on a couch in the dark of a sound-proof cubicle. Four bare walls, a carpet on the floor, a couch wide enough for two. Seventh Jill curled up in the space beside Ngmah, her head buried in Ngmah's lap. In the waiting room outside the cubicle Fifth James and Sixth Michael both unshaved and in shirtsleeves and loosened ties sat on the wide window ledge, talked in whispers among themselves.

The windows of the waiting room overlooked a huge electric power system constructed of thick red brick and corrugated shapes. Three towering chimneys painted red, white and blue belched puffs of black smoke. Embedded on the face of the brick facade, a clock told the time. The river flowed gray in the morning, white in the noon sun and red at sundown. Barges crept upon it upstream and downstream carrying mountains of gravel, cement, coal dust. A parking lot stretched over three square blocks. It was always nearly full both night and day.

First Nancy, Second Katherine, Third Christine, Fourth Jane, though they sat together in another part of the waiting room, did not speak to each other, were oblivious of each other.

The door to Ngmah's cubicle burst open. Seventh Jill, hair hanging loose to the waist, emerged barefoot and blinked in the light. Without a word she ran through the waiting room, ran past the elevators, flung open the door that led into the corridor, ran past his closed door, ran the length of the U-shaped corridor and ran all the way back to where she started from. She stopped short before the door of the cubicle, reentered the dark, climbed back on the couch by Ngmah's side, curled up her legs and placed her head back on Ngmah's lap.

Fifth James and Sixth Michael got up from the window ledge.

Who wants coffee? We are going downstairs for coffee.

*S*undown after supper dishes had been cleared away by the women and stacked to dry by the sink, Seventh Jill practiced Telemann at the piano, Second Katherine having put her child to bed hung out wet laundry on the line strung between the two cherry trees in the back kitchen garden, Dyadya went into his study to read and doze, Ngmah took her twilight stroll at the extreme end of the garden where fruit trees grew—apples, pears, apricots—on land that sloped toward the entrance driveway edged by thick beds of iris and tiger lilies. From there she made her way to her rock garden, a mound rising on the flat lawn halfway between the two giant willows and the fruit trees. In pockets of earth scattered among granite boulders and smaller rocks clumps of mosses grew among periwinkles, dwarf marigolds, viola and angelica. Chicken coop wiring two feet high and all around fenced out rabbits.

She sat on the unmade bed propped against the wicker headboard, her back to the window. On her lap lay an open book. The sun poured through the leaves of the Judas tree outside the window. She heard the boys whispering in the next room.

During the afternoon they had driven off in the green Chevy. She heard the tires whisper discreetly over the gravel driveway, while she, Dyadya and Ngmah were building a wooden rigging for bean vines to climb on at the end of the vegetable garden dug out of a part of a field. Rye gone wild still grew in the field, hiding the short stubby trunks of Norwegian pines, seedlings which Dyadya originally planted and watched grow from year to year. The square bean patch, prepared by gardeners according to Dyadya's specifications, consisted of seven furrows dug from end to end and wooden stakes six feet tall driven into the ground at each corner and in the center of each of the four sides. He had dropped seeds in the furrows while Ngmah followed behind to cover them with loose dark soil. They assembled a collection of stray branches and twigs gathered on the farther end of the rye field along the bridle path on the edge of their land used by riders only in fall and winter when the house was shut as a shortcut back to the stables hidden somewhere beyond the rye and the edge of the woods.

The boys returned at supper time in the Chevy when the bean arbor had just been completed. A strange structure of vertical poles and horizontal branches and twigs tied together by a variety of hemp cord and cotton strings, a structure that had the unmistakable feel and stamp of a rural scene, neat and frugal, from a scroll depicting communal farming, sowing, reaping, fishing, threshing, weaving, tea drinking and the contemplative scholar in his mountain retreat.

Fifth James stalked by her door armed with the shotgun which he and Sixth Michael used for target practice. Sixth Michael remained in his room, tuned his guitar and began to sing. Don't sing love songs You'll wake my mother She's sleeping here . . .

She heard the signal, a single long low whistled note from somewhere below, outside the bathroom window she shared with the boys, repeated three times and interrupting Sixth Michael in midsong. Michael answered the whistle on a higher note and went past her doorway, barefoot and head lowered toting a shotgun in one hand. She heard the rapid thud of his steps descending the back stairway. With a screech and a bang the laundry room door swung open and shut.

She got off the bed and listened by the open doorway for the crack of a gunshot. Instead she heard a series of detonations dulled by distance which could have come from the direction of the highway where men had been working all summer to widen the lanes. But the men normally halted work promptly at three in the afternoon.

She went down the back stairs and passing the breakfast room heard Seventh Jill practicing scales and trills at the piano. In the laundry room, two white deepbellied porcelain sinks were piled high with cut gladioli, salmon, white and pink and purple.

The sun settled above the treetops of the woods beyond the rye field. Dyadya stood in the vegetable garden, hose in hand, near the freshly planted beans. The thin fine spray arched silver against the gray sky swarming with insects. A blackbird cawed three times, flew from the direction of the fruit trees, circled the vegetable plot and disappeared behind the woods.

She climbed the fence and came close to him, out of the path of the spray. The green garden hose trailed serpentine behind him, looped over the fence, uncoiled on the grass and straightened out in widening loops. At the very end, a metal screw connected it to the water sprinkler half hidden by the tumble of flowering rosebush by the fence. Shifting his fingers over the mouth of the hose he was able to control and regulate the force and direction of the spray.

I have watered the entire plot. Water after sundown or else water on plants reflecting the sun's rays will burn and shrivel leaves and petals.

A mosquito bit her leg.

I'll go now Dyadya.

She hesitated an instant to give him a chance, if he should want, to say something else, not to leave him abruptly. She climbed over the fence to the lawn side and saw Ngmah in the distance pulling weeds by the edge of the rock garden. She threw clumps of weeds into the air and they landed pell mell in a shower of loose earth on otherwise immaculate lawn.

She found them silhouetted against the round red sun between the birch grove and the iris and tiger lily beds. At their feet gaped a hole and a black steel trap torn out of the hole. One of them held a thick two-pronged fork aloft, a part of the trap, on the tips of which was impaled a small inert thing that was dark and furry and dead.

*S*he returned from the washroom after waiting out the night sprawled in an armchair in the darkened waiting room. The others who attended vigil had gone below to breakfast in the cafeteria. In the waiting room she found her seated alone by the window, her figure in a bright flower printed dress bathed in a flood of morning sunlight.

Hello. I heard you were back.

For an instant she was unable to grasp what the other was doing seated there sprung out of nowhere. But recovering she answered mechanically Yes I've been back more than a week.

Did you have a good time?

Well I didn't stay long enough to find out. Are you working now?

Really! How could anyone expect me to be working at a time like this. Don't you know I've just had a baby? She pulled down her skirt in exasperation.

Oh yes of course. Congratulations.

They both stared intently away from each other.

You must come and visit us.

I should love that. Are you looking for James? You'll find him with the others downstairs in the cafeteria. They're all having breakfast.

I'm waiting for the nurses to finish up. I've come to see Dyadya.

She stepped forward, took a seat that faced slightly away from the other, and averting her eyes from the blinding glare of the sun, she also waited.

I would have come sooner but having just had the baby I couldn't manage till now. I had a terrible time in the hospital. Dyadya came to see me and the baby. He was very pleased and proud.

She winced hearing the name for the second time.

Oh good. I'm sure he was.

The other got up saying Well I'll go and see Dyadya now. Do come and visit us. Good-bye.

She followed her into the corridor and found her in the room bending over his bed. In full possession of the scene she was whispering in his ear. He did not open his eyes so she said in a hushed voice We'd better leave him he's asleep, but the other replied Why don't you leave I want to stay and leaned closer over him and continued to whisper.

She laid a hand on top of his inert hands that were clasped close to the heaving breathing mechanism jutting out of the slit in his throat and began to rub and knead the back of his hand in rapid fluttering motions like hummingbird wings beating the air. She stopped the movement once to bend her head to his ear and whisper. Still he did not open his eyes and again she rubbed the back of his hand with the tips of her birdlike fingers so that his hands and arms trembled from the onslaught of her fierce persistence.

What are you doing to him!

The other stepped away from the bed and rushed out of the room. He did not move or open his eyes.

*T*he boys took their meals separately behind the closed door of the dining room with blond Scots amah an hour earlier than the girls who ate with their Austrian. The girls would tiptoe up to the closed door to peep through the keyhole, while the Austrian's back was turned. All they could see was blond Scots amah in white uniform raising a fork to her mouth under the lights of the chandelier.

Ngmah held James bundled and bonneted upright in her arms. Her face glowed with fierce pride at presenting to all comers her long-awaited firstborn male whose features resembled hers. Michael perched on a high stool, frowned. His hands held on to the edge of the seat as if to keep from tumbling off.

James and Michael sat side by side on a white over-stuffed sofa. Both were dressed in identical short pants and long-sleeved sweaters, heavy woollen kneesocks and polished leather shoes laced up the center. James held open the pages of a Chinese comic strip book with Chinese words formed in the balloons. Timid and eager Michael peered over the other's shoulder for his share.

Wearing a heavy winter overcoat and in golfer's cap and golfer's ribbed stockings sat Dyadya on a park bench cradling James in the crook of his arm. James's head rested firmly on Dyadya's heart, the length of his body embraced in Dyadya's arm. Fields and woods lay behind them. By the side of the bench stood a bare gnarled tree.

It was First Nancy's turn. She proffered her head under the light. Ngmah bent over to look in her ear. She held a small metal rod the size of a crochet hook but instead of the hook at the end there was a tiny spoon-shaped tip no bigger than a seed pearl. With this instrument she gently loosened and pried out the wax sticking to the walls of the ear. Jubilation when a chunky fragment came up, paper thin fragments veined like wings of flies. Sometimes she lost it in the unreachable recesses of the ear. Then it was Second Katherine's turn. If Ngmah had any patience left she took on the rest according to preference.

Ngmah why not me, why not me?

She knocked at the door.

May I come in?

Michael waited for James to answer.

If you like.

I'll take out your ear wax if you will do the same for me.

As you like.

Can you see? Do you have enough light?

Yes.

She felt the gentle tickling sensation of the hairpin on the walls of her ear then a sharp pain. She shied and tossed her head. The pin dropped to the floor. She nursed her ear by pressing the lobe hard against the opening.

What happened? Did you let the pin drop in my ear?

Yes.

Why?

I was bored. I didn't want to continue.

He walked away from her, sat down at his desk by the window, opened a book and began to read.

Seventh Jill peered around the half-open door and found a nurse.

May we come in?

Naked and inert under the sheet which barely covered him, he seemed unusually huge spread out on the damp wooden board smeared with dark stains that rested on the mattress. A different breathing machine of green plastic with a white curving rubber hose was planted in his throat. The slit where the machine entered was uncovered showing the bare wound. Tubes grew from his legs, thighs and from his arms which were bound at the wrist and pinned to the metal bars of the bed by wide straps of leather. At the foot of the bed stood a round disk-shaped thing that connected, somehow, somewhere to his body ticked off the beats of his heart. Each tick showed up in a short orange light that formed a single jagged line across the face of the disk. The line traveled left to right then disappeared only to reappear at the left. Currents of cold air swept around his bed.

Seventh Jill undid one clenched fist and placed her hand in his hand. The others entered for a time, touched his body, held his other hand, then went out and returned, except Jill who would not relinquish her hand from his until dawn when the disk still ticked out the beats of his heart.

She dashed out with half an hour to spare to fetch fresh sea urchins at a stall two streets from her house because he devoured creatures of the sea he had told her. Not only oysters and clams but especially sea urchins their digestive systems palpable and visible, blood and vomit, the salt clay taste of the sea. She carried the red metal tray filled with layers of crushed ice and seaweeds and two dozen bristling sea urchins, their tops cut away, compartmented sections cut crossways like an orange, exposing grainy orange matter and soft slithering ooze that must have been digestive systems, blood and vomit.

As she stepped into the courtyard of her building she saw him come out of the doorway, his shoulders hunched under his winter coat, his eyes frowning and downcast. He did not look up until she called out his name.

You've come earlier than I expected. It's three minutes before the hour.

He did not reply.

In the elevator she looked up at him.

To think that we almost missed each other. How happy I am to see you. Why didn't you wait for me? My fault, I should have left a note on the door.

You know it's all the same to me if you are home or not. I always have something else to do.

A package lay on the mat propped against her door. Someone left me a package.

I left it. I didn't want to carry it around with me.

What is it?

It's for you.

The package contained a bottle of vinegar, coffee and rock sugar.

They sat down to eat the sea urchins. She ate one and left the rest for him.

Don't you like it?

It tastes like sweetened clay. I can't eat it.

*T*ravel-worn suitcases were piled up high the larger ones sagging at the bottom, against the corridor wall outside Ngmah's bedroom that used to be hers. The walls of the corridor were painted eggshell white which used to be the color before the renovation and the faded blue runner carpet along the center length of the corridor, the floor showing bare at either side, was powder tracked by footprints. Outside the room she was now using which used to be James and Michael's room she recognized her own canvas suitcases piled against the eggshell wall. The doorbell rang.

Who is at the door?

She had been away long enough so that she could no longer tell the difference between the front doorbell and the back doorbell. The back door being closer, the back corridor running parallel to the main just a step away from the door connecting the two arteries, she stepped up to the back door and unlatched the short chain from the catch and opened it. She found no one at the back. The service elevator door was shut. She looked out on the landing and the stairs below. If there had been a delivery the elevator man by rules of the house made since the burglary was required to stand by until delivery had been effected and the tenant's door closed.

Slung across the width of an exposed water pipe jutting out of the wall of the landing she saw a glint of metal, her bracelet of looped anchor chains. Retrieving the bracelet she touched the pipe which was covered with fresh white paint. Her fingers and the bracelet were smeared with it. She reentered the back corridor, pulled shut the door and relatched the chain.

She wandered down the corridor and out into the hall. Through the doorway of the dining room she saw him seated in profile on the wide side of the dining room table, his face turned toward the plumed birds trapped in white cages on the palm fronded wallpaper. Beside him sat Seventh Jill. Scissors in hand she was cutting a length of paper dolls one connected to the next by arms and legs so many had already been cut that the first doll trailed on the blue carpet.

His open eyes looked nowhere, saw nothing. The palms of his hands rested firmly on the table edge and he held his arms close to his sides. She approached and picked up one of his hands and kissed it. She reached up to embrace him by the neck and nestling her cheek against his felt hard bones protruding through his skin.

You are back.

I did not die but only pretended so that I should get some rest, I was so tired. That was the only way I could get some sleep.

How did you manage it?

I kept still in my coffin until everyone had left. Then I unlatched the coffin and crossed by ferry to the farther shore. I stayed in a rooming house facing the sea and I rested. The sky was full of seagulls.

Welcome home Dyadya.

Ngmah entered and took a seat opposite him. She clasped her hands together in her lap and sat erect and still.

Welcome home.

Seventh Jill, seemingly oblivious, continued to cut out paper dolls.

She was sure he had said his work would be over by five-thirty after which time he would come. At six-thirty she telephoned his office only to be told he was not there. She regretted having gone out for bread at five even though she had stuck a note on her door. He must have come, rung her doorbell, seen the note and had not felt like waiting. Or perhaps he had not seen the note, had come to the door, rung the bell without having turned on the hall light.

She opened the double windows of the living room

and clung to the wet railing to look for him in the wind in the rainy streets glittering under street lamps. She shivered from the cold, and went into the bedroom for a jacket, then returned to the window. The possibility that he might have entered her building while she was getting her jacket made her step back from the window, and she ran to unbolt the front door. She remained on the threshold of the doorway. Light from her apartment lit up a patch of the dark hall. A numeral in the panel above the elevator flashed on. The light traveled from the ground floor, passed the first, paused briefly at the second. Then it continued to move upward and, without stopping at her floor, came to rest two floors above. She went inside the apartment and shut the door after her.

She sat through it three times, twice alone and the third time with Michael on a day they had dinner together. The first two times she found herself weeping just before the lights came on.

At sundown the man stood in front of his homestead a rifle gripped in both hands. Before him stretched flat endless deserts dotted by clumps of sagebrush. A canine answered the wail of another. Framed in the dark doorway of the adobe house behind him, the woman also listened. Without turning his head he made a terse signal to the woman, his guarded look never strayed from the increasingly purple landscape.

She went inside and extinguished the lamp that hung by a cord from the ceiling beam. In the corner on the pounded clay floor two children played with a rag doll.

Hush. Hide.

The older child slipped through the rear door and disappeared in the dark. The woman grabbed the younger one from the floor, scooped up the doll and also disappeared through the same door. She reentered alone. She shut and barred the door, closed the flimsy shutters of the two narrow windows and barred them also. She reached above a basin piled high with unwashed dishes of rough pottery and took down from a ceiling beam a long rifle.

The canine calls started again, howl answering howl, frequent and increasing in urgency. The man retreated, taking backward steps to the darkened house, his face always facing the desert.

Under the sagebrush the child held tight her doll and looked up at the feathered warrior crouched above her, pitched against the darkness. She allowed herself to be picked up in his arms but held firm to her doll.

A rider reined his horse, narrowed his eyes under blinding sun, saw wisps of black smoke, blackbirds wheeling in the sky. He urged the horse forward till he came upon the roofless house and smoke-blackened walls. He dismounted entered and reemerged an instant later, reeling and retching.

He rode across the desert in the noonday sun in snow and across plains swept under wind over rock mountains and tree valleys, following and keeping careful distance the child's wanderings. One day he finally entered their camp, dogs yelping, to retrieve the child by bargain. Inside the tent they said after all these years she did not wish to go she had become one of them. The elder child's hair hung on a trophy stick beside the hair of the man who held the gun and the woman who extinguished the lights.

He was midway across the stream when she came stumbling down the embankment, half child half woman. She looked at him without recognition when he spoke her name.

You remember me. I held you I gave you the doll.

She stood paralyzed her eyes never leaving him.

Cross. You don't belong there. You belong with us.

She looked at him, advanced a few steps toward the edge of the stream, retreated a few steps. A commotion of dogs and men came within hearing. He spurred his horse gathered her up by the waist and hoisted her to the front of his saddle. The horse dashed forward and reached the other side of the shore.

A woman stood on the porch of an adobe house, shaded her eyes with a hand to better see through the haze shimmering over the desert. She saw a slow moving speck coming toward her. He approached with the child woman clumsily wrapped in a blanket and cushioned against the saddle and in the crook of his arm.

I have brought her home.

The lights came on.

Sixth Michael got up from his seat to let someone pass.

Shall we go?

She did not answer him.

Why are you crying?

Michael do you mind if we sit through it once more?

Just once more or maybe halfway.

I have a quiz tomorrow.

Well, just to see how the house looked in the very beginning. You haven't seen it. We'll leave when you've seen it.

All right.

He took her home which he would have done anyway. But because it was late and dark and cold, the streets slippery with ice and huge embankments of frozen snow not yet removed at unfrequented crossings along their way, and because she had just left the hospital that week he took special care to help her across the snowy streets, listened attentively to her breathless incoherent chatter and at the doorway of the house where she lived alone said sweetly and gently good night to her.

*T*he ringing of the telephone woke her. She got out of bed and went to his room at the end of the corridor to pick up the extension.

Come quickly. He's bleeding again. It started while I was in the country to pick flowers for him.

He needed blood, fresh and preferably from a member of the family. Seventh Jill had it but had left that morning to return to school across the continent. Michael who had also left did not have it. When she arrived everyone had already been tested but did not have it. She took the test. She had it.

He watched his blood leave his body segment by segment moving in relentless darts through the tube inserted in his nostril, losing more than he could take in.

They attached the last bottle on the rod by his bedside. She bent down and kissed his hand.

My blood Dyadya.

He grasped her hand tightly, enveloping it with both his hands and wrung it fervently, in quick abrupt shakes, a gesture demonstrating feeling and gratitude customary among some Chinese of the old school.

It's yours Dyadya.

She listened to the steady ticks of the disk at the foot of his bed.

He released her hand and continued to observe the rate at which blood flowed out of his body into the tube.

He sat with shoulders hunched, arms and elbows resting on the glass-topped breakfast table in the kitchen, having finished his breakfast of rice porridge, soft-boiled eggs, pickled vegetable and steamed anchovies.

Behind him in the shadow of the laundry room amah hung out dustcloths, wide squares of limp cheesecloth spread out to dry like fishermen's fine nets like shrouds laid on top of each other on all the rungs of the two racks that slid out of the wall on runners. Underneath the racks in the wall were gas burners which black amah used to light when she came to do laundry twice a week before the children left home.

Ngmah entered the laundry room by way of the back corridor.

I am not feeling well.

Shall we go out to the country today? The sky is a brilliant blue. The begonias and the jessamines must be out by now, the Judas tree bursting, apple blossoms falling. I want to see if the gardener's crew has trimmed the Japanese maple and cut the grass along the borders of the driveway. Surely you will want to see how your peonies are making out and I want to do some planting.

I am not feeling well. I don't want to go.

The air will do you good. Don't stay home and brood.

He pushed back his chair to get up. He opened the wall installed freezer where bread was kept wrapped in wax paper. Slips of ice from the wrapper fell on the floor.

Must you mess up the floor. Amah mopped the floor late into the night and stayed up until midnight to finish the work. Amah clean it up. I must keep the floor clean.

He did not reply but opened the icebox above the freezer, took out two jars of jam which he placed beside the toaster together with the bread. Ngmah made the jam from recipes she had learned when she took a course one year in home economics at Teachers College of Columbia University.

Amah turned on the taps in one of the laundry basins, picked out a mop from a collection stashed in a corner of the laundry room and soaked it. She closed the taps and squeezed out the water from the mop. She mopped the floor, starting first with the laundry room, then the kitchen and the pantry. Several times she returned to the basin to rinse out the mop.

While he waited for the bread to pop out of the toaster, her gliding mop neared his feet, but he did not budge. The toast popped. He glanced down at the damp surface about him, took off his slippers and stepped gingerly toward the icebox in his stockinged feet. Ngmah seated at the table watched all his movements. He took out a roll of butter, returned to his original position by the toaster and began to butter the toast.

You are dropping crumbs on the counter. Amah cleaned the counter until midnight last night.

What is the matter with you?

You have seen her I know you have I feel it. Admit it.

Why should I hide it. I have seen them both. I want to help him he is my son. Here, eat the toast I am making for you. You don't eat a balanced diet. It will do you good. And then we will go to the country.

I don't want any toast.

What do you want?

I want him back but without her.

She stamped her feet, pushed away the plate of toast and fled from the house on the road along the edge of the canal where silks floated heavily in water for the dye to set. Thirst and hunger, hunger Father. She stood in front of the wash basin in her bathroom. Scrutinizing the image in the mirror she heard him shatter a dish on the floor of the kitchen.

The macadam road leading from the railway station on the outskirts of the city led to the main gate of the house. Along that road he planted trees on both sides, poplar saplings spaced twenty feet apart. The rickshaw runner pulled them in a leisurely jog home from Miss Ironside's school.

Ngmah went out alone by train to the country and went into the garden to cut button chrysanthemums the first of the season, bright reds purples whites yellows which they had planted together in early summer. She brought them back wet, in a shallow straw basket in the chill of late afternoon to the waiting room and mixed sprays of color to paint a picture for him. She entered his room and presented him the flowers she had picked alone in the garden. He looked at the flowers for a long time. A tear from his unblinking eyes slid slowly down a crease above his cheek.

*T*he nurse on duty ran out into the waiting room.

Come quickly. He is awake and is trying to say something.

She ran into his room ahead of the nurse. His arms were no longer strapped to the bars and he flailed them in the air searching for a hold to stop from sinking. Wide tormented eyes stared into nothing. Under the untucked sheets the body bandaged and tubed and bound thrashed and heaved on the mattress. A nurse held him down another steadied the machine in his throat. He opened and closed his mouth gasping for air. She found his hands and kissed them. He paused his struggle, turned his head and focused his eyes. His lips formed the word Jill.

She's coming.

Michael?

He's coming.

His lips formed another word.

Love.

His hands she gathered made stabbing motions of emphasis, stabbing at her. He turned away and closed his eyes. She let go his hands, walked to the end of the bed and leaned over still as he. Then she covered his cold feet under the two fronts of her unbuttoned jacket and placed her heart against his feet.

*A*lready a week had passed since she posted the letter inviting him to eat duck that she would prepare and cook in a rather special way. In her letter she even described how. There was no word from him by letter or telephone so she called his office in the morning again in the afternoon and each time was told by the operator that he was absent but was expected to drop by during the course of the day.

In order to do the ducks properly they ought to be marinated twenty-fours hours in advance of cooking. But she felt reluctant to take them still wrapped up in paper and tied neatly with strings from the icebox for fear that after all the trouble he might not come for the meal. It seemed ludicrous that she should sit down to a solitary feast. She could not bear the thought of it.

She got out of her bath, carried a pile of back issues of his newspaper to the bedroom and got into bed. It had become her habit to reread his articles before turning out the light, paying particular attention to passages she had underlined. Descriptions of gestures or ideas or words which appeared familiar though they functioned in quite different contexts, words, gestures, ideas which had taken place during the brief space and time they had been together. These words, phrases, paragraphs she isolated from their public meaning and context since by setting them apart she was able to dote more easily on their private sense, memory arousing such as his reference to an undressable mistress. For her it meant something other than the use he made of it to describe the film under discussion and she nursed and cherished words, phrases, paragraphs during long periods of his silence and his absence.

She woke up agitated and wide awake in the middle of the night. Were he really to appear for lunch, the ducks would not be ready, there would be nothing for him to eat. She got out of bed, turned on the light in the hall, leaving the door open between kitchen and hall. She washed the ducks quietly under a thin warm jet of water and left them to drain propped against the side of the sink. The marinade she made by measuring into a pot honey, salt and pepper, crushed ginger and garlic, chopped scallions, soya sauce and generous pourings of sherry and bourbon. She brought the contents of the pot to a boil, stirred for several minutes then turned out the flame. She dried the ducks with paper towels, placed them in a deep earthenware dish and poured over them the dark steaming liquid from the pot. She covered the ducks with aluminum foil tucked tightly around the rim of the dish, opened the kitchen window, turned out the light in the hall and went back to bed.

In the morning she took a bus to the other end of the city to fetch a copy of the *Tao Te Ching* very excellently translated in his language which she had ordered for him. Then she went to another part of the city to buy a bottle of bourbon which could be found in only one place, in a shop close to his office. The last time he came she had offered him Scotch. He had said he preferred bourbon.

Her instinct which told her he would come that day aroused her to a pitch of efficiency and she was impatient to go out to perform errands which normally fazed her. On certain days moving from one room to another in her apartment was the only displacement she felt capable of undertaking. She was used to being alone with her thoughts so that hearing another language spoken on the street frequently shocked and unnerved her. Then again she found it maddening that for milk she had to go to one place, for meat to another, vegetables elsewhere, coffee across the street, soap up the street, bread down the street, cigarettes somewhere else and always having to wait in line.

That day was different. With no effort and with no tarrying she left the apartment for the second time, having already put the ducks in the oven. She left the book and the bottle of bourbon on the table in the hall and went out to finish the rest of her marketing. Trajectories she made from shop to shop related to him were a succession of offerings to him. Heading back weighed down by a loaded basket and a net string bag bulging with produce she rehearsed in her mind stories to tell him, questions to ask him, something to show, something to delight him, something to say to him so that he should feel the world larger in her presence.

She left her door open, taking care to draw the bolt so that it would not shut accidentally in case she should not hear the doorbell while washing and draining the spinach. The noon sun entering full force through the kitchen window made bright the space around the two sinks. She soaked the unwashed leaves in one sink then transferred selected leaves for a more thorough washing into the adjoining sink.

When the doorbell rang she called out to him, turned off the tap, and went out to meet him.

He held her in a tightening grip till she cried out. He released her and she clung to him.

Among your lovers am I your favorite?

She felt his grip tighten again and broke away from him. She picked up the book lying on the hall table.

It's for you.

Wonderful. Just the thing I need to read at night. Better than reading detective stories before going to bed.

It's the very best translation in your language. You should start reading from the back and go forward.

What does it say here?

Tao ken tao fei chang tao.

What does it mean?

The translation is on the facing page.

Min ken min fei . . .

Stop. No time now. We'll read it together on the train this afternoon. Do you want to come with me? I am giving a talk out of town this evening.

I'd like to go. Is it far?

About three hours from here by train. The train leaves at six. I have to leave you at three. I have things to do and appointments to keep.

Never leave me.

You shouldn't have said that. I am leaving this very instant.

Why?

I told you never to ask why. You must always be amusing and sweet and never ask why. So then, what have you been doing with yourself?

During your absence . . .

I'm leaving. You're really impossible.

She shrugged her shoulders and went into the kitchen to take out the spinach from its second soaking which she piled on the drainboard.

Would you like a drink?

No. Americans drink too much. Besides I only like bourbon.

She came back from the hallway with the bottle of bourbon wrapped and tied with a bow at the neck. Smiling triumphantly she set it in front of him.

For you. Very special.

He smiled while he undid the wrapping. It pleased her to see him reach up to the cupboard, quite at ease in her kitchen and pick out a glass on the shelf. He poured and took a sip, then turned the bottle around to read the label pasted on the back.

The water roared down the drain. She put the stopper back into the hole and turned on the cold tap to re-fill the sink. He stood behind her as she sorted out the rotten leaves which she discarded. The good she kept adding to the growing pile on the drainboard.

He placed his hands on her shoulders and began to kiss her behind the ears and on the back of the neck. In an attempt to kiss her farther down the neck, he pulled and tugged at the collar of her turtleneck sweater which refused to give way. Finally he tugged very hard and succeeded in planting a kiss between her shoulder blades.

You're choking me.

Coughing and laughing she bent back her head and kissed him on his cheek. He returned to sit by the table.

She opened the oven door, basted the ducks, turned the dial a notch lower and closed the oven. She climbed up a chair to take down a large frying pan from an upper shelf of the cupboard. While she was getting off the chair he put his hand on her knee. She placed the pot on top of the stove and lit the burner underneath.

Stretched out on the floor of the hall just in front of the kitchen door he read the international edition of *The New York Times*. At the threshold of the kitchen she crouched down and reached out to touch his hair.

Anything interesting in today's paper? Can you understand? I bought some magazines this morning which I thought you might like to read. They're on the couch in the living room.

I've seen them. I read them all yesterday at the hairdresser.

He turned a page of the *Times*, shaking his head in disapproval.

What's the matter?

Stupid newspaper and reactionary besides.

She laughed.

In certain circles in America it is considered almost left.

He turned over another page.

You should return to China.

What for?

America is not your country. You should work for China.

What could I do there? I'm not good at ditch digging.

You could do something in the area of finance.

I know a little about the stock market but I doubt whether it's an interest the present government would encourage.

You have to go back. You have no future in America. You are an exile in America as you are in exile here.

I am in exile here voluntarily in order to rest, to remove myself from ties for the moment.

China would welcome you with open arms.

Don't be simple-minded. What makes you think so?

Because you're Chinese.

I needn't be told that. But that is no reason for going back. Besides once I enter it's unlikely I'll be able to get out. You forget I am also American.

You're not.

Well then, let's say I wouldn't be able to see you and have lunch with you again. Not that I see much of you as it is.

You can always read my articles. There'll be messages for you only you can decipher because it will be between us.

I couldn't live without America. It's a part of me by now. For years I used to think I was dying in America because I could not have China. Quite unexpectedly one day it ended when I realized I had it in me and not being able to be there physically no longer mattered. Those wasted years when I denied America because I had lost China. In my mind I expelled myself from both.

You must be out of your mind. I don't understand a word you're saying.

I express myself badly.

Not the words, but the ideas are foolish.

I'll try again. When it had been possible to return to China while still living in America I loved America and

China as two separate but equal realities of my existence. Before the outbreak of civil war in China I lived for the day when I could bring America with me to China. Selfishly I wanted both my worlds. In the early days of civil warfare I waited hopefully, impatiently for a sign that China would eventually be recognized so that I could return with my America. It didn't seem possible that she would be unrecognized indefinitely. The government was effectively and authentically in control, was qualified for the job, so to speak. It had achieved unity, the lack of which during the last one hundred years blocked China's life and life's plenitude. Since she belonged to me I wanted her to live so that I might live America there as I had lived China in America. I wanted China, it had the potential to have a true place in the world to become another America in the sense that America is a good place to live for oneself and for others, to live fully, with dignity, and to work in the main current of life.

Our engagement in Korea paralyzed me. I saw with dread my two lives ebbing. Each additional day of estrangement increased the difficulty of eventual reconciliation, knowing the inflexibility of Chinese pride. In that paralysis I lived in no man's land, having also lost America since the loss of one entailed the loss of the other. Moments I thought of giving up one for the other, I had such longings to make a rumble in the silence. But both parts equally strong canceled out choice. What makes me so talkative today? I should be feeding you lunch.

I don't come here for lunch. I come here to learn and be amused.

The butter sizzled in the frying pan. He watched attentively as she added handfuls of spinach not completely dry into the hot butter sputtering in the pan. As leaves darkened and shrank she continued to add fresh handfuls, stirring constantly and turning over the entire supply of spinach simmering gently in its own juices in the pan.

Is lunch ready? What time is it?

She opened the door of the oven and turned over the ducks so that the undersides faced the grill.

No not yet.

She followed him into the bedroom after putting a lid on the spinach and sat on the edge of the bed next to his reclining figure. She raised his head with some effort and slipped another pillow underneath.

There. Be pasha in my house.

You're always busy cooking whenever I come. It's not much fun.

I started too late because I wasn't sure you would come.

I have to leave at three.

It's half-past one now. We'll eat at two. Don't move. I'll be right back. I want to look at the spinach.

He let out a sigh of exasperation.

She gave the spinach one more stir, turned out the fire, covered the pan and went back to the bedroom.

Shall I tell you a story while we wait for lunch?

One evening she visited Dyadya and found in his

study a magazine sent from China. On the first page was a poorly reproduced photograph of a farmer's house built up of mud and rushes and roofed in tile standing in the middle of a neatly tilled field. A tree clung by the wall of the house, a line of mountains beyond the fields. With a shock she recognized the landscape, could smell the tilled soil, felt the embrace of the house, climbed the mountains. Unguarded, a seizure of loss struck her. For an instant she could not breathe.

Late at night in her own apartment it was hot and she could not sleep. She finally pulled off the sheets from the bed and went out to the living room which was weakly air conditioned. She spread the sheets on the couch and fell asleep.

The lights were on when she woke up. She saw white walls, ceiling, floor, some furniture about but did not know where she was. Certainly this must be death she thought. How strange yet natural to wake up dead with white walls, ceiling, floor and pieces of furniture scattered about. She had managed to enter death wrapped in white sheets, a crossing not so difficult as one would imagine. She marveled at the lack of fuss.

She became aware of the dull whir of motors. It seemed unusual yet natural that air conditioning came with death. Then she heard a sound which she recognized gradually as trickles of water dripping from the air conditioner. She remembered how she came to this room and felt somehow unrelieved by the waking.

He stared at her when she finished.

Well, did you like the story?

Live in China.

Too late now. Farm house, field, solitary tree, the distant mountains have fused, have become one with the American landscape. I can't separate any more. If I were to live in China today I would have to conceal one half of myself. In America I need not hide what I am.

You have betrayed China.

What makes you neutrals so anti-American? I belong to both, am both.

She took out the ducks from the oven and placed them on a platter without bothering to make any sauce since there was no time. She set two places on the kitchen table and served him spinach while he carved the ducks. They ate the meal in silence.

Have I put you in a bad mood?

It's past three. I have to leave.

He got up, picked up the book and also his coat folded in two on the hall table.

May I come with you? What time are you leaving?

At about five.

Shall I be able to reach you at the office?

You can always try. Leave a message.

What about the bourbon?

Save it for me.

She called at four and left a message, and again at half-past. In the evening when she took off her sweater before going to bed she found threads and stitches torn and unraveled around the rim of the neckline.

*H*e brought back one year asparagus from the greenhouse to plant in the deep well-dug bed of drained soil lightened with coarse sand prepared early in winter the year before. He had added lime to cut soil acidity and had been generous with fertilizer at the rate of three ounces per yard. He had covered the ground with peat moss and in February had forked the site and now again in spring at planting time.

He dug trenches fifteen inches wide and eight inches

deep with a ridge three to four inches high down the center of the trench. He placed plants on top of this ridge at intervals of fifteen to eighteen inches, carefully spreading out the roots of each plant. With his bare hands he worked the soil through and over the roots to a depth of two inches above the crowns and subsequently filled the trenches gradually.

In fall when the bed was rife with fernlike foliage he cut the stems a few inches from the surface and mounded up the soil a few inches deep over the crowns. Then he recovered the bed with peat moss.

In the dream she knew she was dreaming, seated waiting with hands clasped in the tiny kitchen, she looked out as snow fell into the air shaft. The walls of the air shaft were bathed evenly in pale orange light glowing from a higher window which she could not see but knew existed and would see once she came out of her dream. She looked out at the falling snow, large flakes floated across her window like cotton fluffs. In the stillness Fifth James and Sixth Michael came home.

She and Third Christine crossed the dark field to start the planting. A beggar carried in his arms a log tall as a northern pine. Fifth James and Sixth Michael followed the beggar who dropped his load at the edge of the field. She said James and Michael we must pick it up and plant it. She and Chistine shouldered the front end while James and Michael raised the rear. The log was so long that Fifth James and Sixth Michael seemed mere specks at the other end. The weight of the log on their shoulders they ran in straight lines from one end of the field to the other back and forth until the entire field had been planted and the night changed into gray of morning.

The doorbell rang. She stepped dripping out of the bathtub, covered herself with a towel and went to the door. Recognizing the voice from the other side she unbolted the lock.

What are you doing in town on a Sunday?

I often come in on Sundays.

Really?

Yes. To attend afternoon performances at the theater. Sunday afternoon performances are something out of the ordinary. They can be so bad they are hilarious.

Have you come to see a performance today? I had expected you on another day.

She stepped back into the bath, closed her eyes and sank into the water so that only her head showed above the pine-scented foam.

Look here, I got the days confused. I did come on Friday. I heard voices from your apartment and thought you were giving a party.

You must have been mistaken. I never give parties. You were invited for Thursday.

You're falling asleep in the water. Sleep. Don't let me disturb you.

He sat on the covered toilet seat and lit a cigarette.

The trouble you know is that I don't have your telephone number.

I gave it to you once.

I've lost it. Otherwise I would have telephoned.

Would you have?

She drew herself out of the water, reached for a towel hanging by the wall and began drying herself. He took the towel from her and with it brushed off specks of foam clinging to her back.

I can't understand why I mistook the day for Friday.

Neither can I. You even wrote it down on your book.

Did I? The trouble is that I didn't have your telephone number.

He knelt towel in hand to dry her legs. She bent down and kissed him on the forehead.

Suddenly he dashed out to the hall, searched the pockets of his coat and came back with his calendar.

Quick. Tell me what's your number. I'll put it down right now. Tell me quick.

She called out the number while buttoning her robe.

Do you care for a drink?

He shook his head.

She went out into the kitchen and poured a drink for herself. When she came out drink in hand she found him in the bedroom lying on her bed.

Do you want to listen to a record?

What is it?

A Chinese opera.

With sharp clacks of wood on wood followed by nervous clashes of cymbal the opera began. The flourish over, the clack of sticks resumed. Four irregular beats. Each pause in between lasted longer than the one before. A voice stated the action.

What is it about?

It's about a battle. Our army at Ch'i San plains traps Ssu Ma I. A messenger enters. Though man traverses one thousand miles, horse traverses ten thousand miles weaving mountain passes. I bring military map. Beg audience with commander . . .

I am leaving for America in a few days.

A frown creased his face as he raised himself on an elbow to peer at her face. She felt a momentary tightening of his arm clasped around her waist.

How long will you be away?

I haven't made up my mind. Probably for a few weeks. I need a change of scene. Sad to be alone at this time of year. If you hadn't appeared today I wouldn't have seen you again. I had decided not to call or write.

He reached above her body for his pack of cigarettes lying on the lamp table by her side of the bed, lit a cigarette and settled back on the pillows.

You won't come back.

She posed an ashtray on his bare chest. Lying on her stomach, propped on elbows, she kissed his shoulders, then looked at him.

Will you miss me?

He puffed on his cigarette and stared at the ceiling. Percussion rushed into the frantic fray of clacking sticks, the savage turbulence of cymbals and gongs quickening to madness. A sudden halt. The voice broke into the silence, two staccato notes, then a prolonged shriek of rage followed by three single clacks of a wooden clapper. He looked at her.

Is it over?

In sharp measured paces the staccato of clacks resumed. The clash of cymbals, resonance cut short by hands, entered on each fourth off-beat of the sticks. Another halt nicked the flow. Then flutes merged with the rest in wild weaving wails of tearing anguish.

He extinguished his cigarette, set the ashtray on the floor and holding her by the shoulders, kissed her hair and ears.

The opposing commander holds his restive troops outside the gates of the city but does not enter, suspicious of entrapment. In the city another commander looking out from the watch tower, picks up the bipa and plucking its strings laments brooks and meadows and former pleasures of his carefree youth. She moved out of his grasp and turned on her side.

I know you won't come back.

Will you miss me?

Where will you stay?

With relatives. I used to have an apartment. You would have liked it, a tiny place perched in the sky surrounded by a narrow terrace tiled in red brick which I used to hose down after coming home from the office. On the terrace were trees, real trees in wooden buckets, and birds came. One day I took the trees out to the country and replanted them in Father's garden. In good weather I used to cook on that terrace. You know what? I have a great idea.

She heaved herself across his body. His eyes looked apprehensive while she clasped and lightly squeezed his throat with both hands.

What?

We're going to have a picnic.

She gave him a hearty kiss on his cheek, released hold of his neck and sprang out of bed. He followed her into the kitchen where she made a great clatter opening icebox and cupboard doors, cutting meat in slices, opening cans and packages of biscuits.

Oh, pour me something, quick, I'm so excited, I'm going home. There, under the sink.

He took out a bottle of wine from under the sink where the wines were stored and looked about for a corkscrew.

On the counter beside the sink.

She hurried into the bedroom and pulled out a fresh white sheet from the closet which she refolded in the shape of a square, and spread it on the center of the bed, leaving uncovered a bit of the blanket on either side. He brought in the bottle of wine, uncorked, and two empty glasses. Passing him on her way to the kitchen she reached up to kiss him. While she laid platters of cold sliced meats and pickles, plates of biscuits and nuts on the center of the white square, he got under the blanket on one side of the bed and poured out a bit of wine in a glass which he handed her. She sipped.

Aren't you having some?

Not now.

You'd like some toast, wouldn't you? I just happen to have bread today.

Not essential, though it would be nice if you can manage it. How will you do it. Shall I do it?

He threw off the covers and started to get out of bed.

No, I'll put slices of bread under the grill. Won't take me more than a minute. Don't move. I'll be right back.

He opened his mouth in mock despair and tucked his legs back under the cover.

Bent over in front of the open door of the oven she gingerly turned over thick slabs of bread, averting her face from the heat she felt the touch of his hand caress her back, moving hesitantly from the small of her back, up along the spine, dwelling at the arch where neck and shoulders meet. Although she knew he would not reply she asked casually without looking up Do you love me? He did not reply but continued to caress her back.

You won't come back.

She switched off the grill and forked out hot toast onto a plate which he held docile and ready near the mouth of the oven.

Conjugate for me the subjunctive of to live.

Seemingly disconcerted, the movement of his hand paused on the back of her neck.

Don't you know it?

Not all persons. I confuse between present and imperfect.

He walked beside her, his hand on her shoulder, as she carried the plate of toast to the bedroom.

Well?

Of course you know it.

Propped up on the pillows he watched her butter a piece of toast on which she heaped thin slices of steak sprinkled with salt and pepper.

Have you your ticket?

I've reserved a place.

From her perch at the foot of the bed she leaned over the square sheet to hand him a sandwich. She was buttering a second piece of toast when he suddenly conjugated to live in the subjunctive mood. After he finished, she stared at him, then took a bite of toast.

We should live together.

Oh, so that's why you asked. It's not possible.

He watched her intently while she buttered another toast and shook his head when she offered it.

I steal from you, do you know that? Without you I would stop writing. I steal your thoughts, your language, sounds, movements, all, all.

Unprepared to match his candor by confessing her own culpability, she refrained from asking how, in what way.

What would you do if you were to stop writing?

Do nothing or work for myself, not for others. Perhaps make films.

She edged around the folded sheet till she reached him at the head of the bed, touched his face and kissed him.

Close your eyes and open your mouth.

No.

She turned half away, then glanced back.

His eyes, squeezed tightly shut twisted his face into a grimace. He opened his mouth wide, arched his neck, and obediently received a ginger wafer.

What will you do when you are there?

See people, take walks. If I give you my address, will you write?

Perhaps, if you don't stay away too long.

The besieged commander sounded his last note, having defended the city, reluctantly executed erring subordinates, prepared his report to the Throne. Three flourishes of wooden clacks interspersed with strokes of the gong ended the performance. She went to the other room to turn off the machine.

I'll write to let you know when I return.

*W*ho is coming to the party tonight? She asked the question in precise careful English seated with legs crossed and feet resting on the cushion of the opposite chair just vacated by Seventh Jill who went up to the stove to peer over amah's shoulder. She liked to sit in that chair with her back to the laundry room. It gave her a clear view of the entire kitchen, the broad pantry and a section of the dining room.

Ngmah continued to stir the contents of a large open

pot on the stove while amah stood in attendance, clutching in her fingers an assortment of limp potholders.

Silence. This is the first time I am giving a party without him. The terrors I used to feel seem to have happened a long time ago, are now dissipated. Hanging in my cedar-lined closets are dresses none of which fit properly. Always a bit to take in a bit to take out. I long to find a dress that would fit me perfectly. I long to be seen in my perfect-fitting dress.

Who is coming to the party?

Silence. Who will see me in my dress? I see him leaning forward. His hands are resting squarely on his knees in anticipation of rising. The floorboards creak under his hurried tread. He has left his room at the end of the corridor and now makes his way along the dark corridor heading for the pool of light my rooms glow in search of me. We shall go out just the two of us for dinner tonight.

Amah picked up the pot from the stove and set it down to cool in the pantry. She returned to the stove and placed a large clean frying pan on a burner in front of Ngmah.

Who is coming to the party?

Ngmah looked up startled, as though hearing the question for the first time. She spooned a chunk of lard from an open package by the stove, knocked the handle of the spoon sharply against the edge of the rapidly heating pan and waited for the lard to melt.

Let me see now. First Nancy and Second Katherine are coming. And I thought of asking your cousins but it appears they're having a party on the same night. I could not have them all, the way it used to be, since this is the first time I am attempting a gathering without him.

In the laundry room amah huddled over the sink in an attitude of devotion washed rice in a pot. Patient and methodical, her fingers stirred gently in slow circular movement the grains of rice swirling in cold water, her silent conversation with rice and water. Whenever the water clouded she carefully tilted the white enamel pot on its side, letting the water run into the sink. She refilled the pot and discarded the water five times and did not let a single grain escape with the tide. When the water cleared sufficiently so that the rice in the bottom became visible through the water, she added the correct amount of water for cooking. Rice to the height of the first joint of her forefinger. Water measured to the second joint. She put a lid on the pot and carried it to the stove.

Who else is coming?

I explained to your uncle who came a few days before your return, in such a hurry he could not stay more than a minute and left behind a flowering plant which he drew out of a shopping bag. Not a real plant, the petals were colored feathers and the leaves . . .

Who else is coming?

Third Christine is coming with all her babies. We will put them in his room. The bed there is large enough.

Anyone else?

Ngmah threw into the frying pan a handful of

chopped scallions and ginger and over it emptied a bowl of raw shrimps, whole and shells intact. She stood with face averted and waited for the smoke and splattering grease to subside. Then she stirred in sugar, salt and a dash of sherry, covered the pan and lowered the heat.

Silence. The house used to be filled with presents at this time of year. Gifts received and gifts we used to give and I did most of the shopping. Every year somebody used to send a brace of pheasants which took up space on the pantry counter, practically half the counter, that large long carton. Heads, feathers, tails all intact lying on a bed of shiny green plastic curlings. I used to mistake the package for a florist's carton, imagining flowers inside, long-stemmed giant chrysanthemums. I cannot remember who used to send them. Bottles of champagne, wines and liquors. Biscuits and plumcakes, chinaware and ribboned steamer baskets packed tight with fresh fruit and nuts and conserves, silverware and glassware and scores of gloves ties and scarves and sweaters. And that frantic last minute dash to shops before the final holiday closing to buy presents in return for those unexpectedly received.

Have you asked anyone else?

What?

To the party.

Sixth Michael is coming. I have also asked Fifth James.

Have you given in? Is she coming?

Well let me see for this was the way I put it to him. James I am having a party next Thursday night. You are invited to come. I particularly did not mention her name. I did not say I was inviting her though I did say bring the baby.

She's coming then.

I am not so sure. However if she decides to come I did not invite her.

I cannot come.

Ngmah rinsed out the dishcloth and wiped off all traces of grease on the area surrounding the covered frying pan.

Do as you like.

Amah sat apart on a stool under the dim ceiling light over the laundry room. She sat with her back against the door of the washing machine. Her head nodded in sleep. Once her forehead touched the cold enamel of the machine. She woke up thinking it was morning and felt cold and hungry.

Silence. Mornings before he left for the office he used to stop outside my open doorway to peer in then would creep away fearful of awaking me. I would hear him step discreetly into my study. He would leave money on my glass coffee table, bills of tens and twenties, an old habit, in case I should be short for the day and not have time to go round the corner before the bank closed. Crabs are costly today I can scarcely afford them. There is no money on the coffee table.

He came home, took off his hat and placed his leather envelope on the telephone table. I said There is nothing to eat for dinner. I went shopping today and have not had time to prepare anything. He said That is all right, we shall go out for dinner.

I held on to him in the street while waiting for the doorman to find us a cab. At the third whistle a cab drew up and we entered it. We went to a restaurant and I ordered crabs.

My body followed the broad swing of his gait, weaving side by side like a boat tossed on waves. What is that mess on his coat? He looked at a pile of white hairs clinging to the inner part of his sleeve and the front side of his coat near his heart. Laughing I said You silly the hair from my white coat has come off on you. I bought it yesterday I did not know it sheds. He said Expensive coats I buy for expensive ladies shed hairs on me. You should order one with material that does not shed. Well I said I have looked at one today that is of a very rare shade. Every single skin matches perfectly. It is a shade which only I can wear though I can wear rags and get away with it. I can even wear a black pebble on my finger and people will take it for a sapphire. He said Do you want a black sapphire? Perhaps, let me think it over I am not sure if I want it black I want to take a look at what is available. Very good, very good, take a look, and he patted my gloved hand that nestled in the crook of his arm so warm and snuggly there.

Seventh Jill turned away from the night outside the window and faced the room.

It seems to me you cannot live forever not seeing her. There has to be a meeting. She exists.

She has played her role in completing our story. My life from now on is separate from the story which has ended. My life now has no place for her.

Silence. Annoyance stiffened my body when he used to pause in front of shopwindows along our way to examine objects that might serve as suitable presents for First, Second, Third or Fourth. I was so impatient with cold and hunger and thirst standing with him by the window while he took his time looking. But should something happen to catch my eye and I would stop to look he would urge me along as if I were chattel. And if I did not follow fast enough he would dash off like a ship tossing from side to side with each stride, would cross the street before the light changed leaving me stranded on the corner while traffic zoomed left and right. Now I am left alone on the other side of the street. When can I put on my feathers and furs and jewels and descend dazzling each step of the stair? What shall I do with my dowry now that he is gone?

But you cannot avoid her. You are bound to meet. It's not realistic.

Seventh Jill cast down here eyes, embarrassed at having used the word realistic.

You see I cannot bear the end of the story. I cannot bear my part.

We accept her.

We each have a different story with a different ending. The elements are the same, the combinations different.

Silence. Somewhere in the house a window is open. I am cold. My room contains the only window which opens but rarely do I open it because of the dust and dirt. The draft ruffles my newly set hair. You have

strong and good hair said the hairdresser as he took
an apple from the basket of apples which I brought
back from the country. The apples are for those who
serve me. I must wear my white scarf to protect my
hairdo. The draft enters from an open window next to
his room and he is at the wheel of the car. I stare into
the mirror attached to the sun visor which I lower. I
look into it while the darkening countryside flashes
by until it is too late to see I am am I beautiful. He
stopped the car while the headlights beamed on the
closed garage turning the door bright red. I help him
take out provisions from the trunk of the car. He and I
are spending the night in the country.

It is time to dress.

Amah got up from her stool and shuffled out of the
laundry room into the narrow dim corridor leading to
her spare room piled with boxes from floor to ceiling,
boxes filled with his clothing which Ngmah as exorcism
had emptied out of all the drawers and closets of his
room a week after the funeral. She could not have her
dinner until the discussion ended in the kitchen and the
eating began and finished. She wanted to go home. Before leaving she must show that she has taken nothing
from the household, submit her frayed suitcase of lam-
inated paper the lid open for inspection before her departure. You see I have taken nothing. Here is my open
suitcase. Please examine for yourself. I have nothing.

She heard the front door open and close as she walked
out of his room at the end of the corridor. She hurried

toward amah's room, carrying the dress she needed to alter draped over her arm. She did not quite make it in time to her sanctuary but stood aside, her hand on the doorknob while the other, at the heels of the child, swept through the corridor on her way to his room, pausing momentarily to call out hello over her shoulder.

She closed the door and sat down on the edge of amah's bed alongside a narrow window which looked out on a brick wall. She sat down on the bed, threaded her needle and began to sew.

The door to the corridor swung open. A child stood in the doorway and stared inside. Composed, she held her ground, enormous eyes unflinching from the stare of the other. Her stubby child shoes made sharp abrupt thumps on the bare wooden floor as she approached the bed. She stood feet apart, riveted to the floor, directly in front of the other. The mother entered.

Oh, there you are. Hush. And don't touch. Don't touch Aunty's things.

She sat down on the bed.

Well I hear you're keeping yourself busy.

Speech was locked in her heart.

You poor thing do you feel better now?

Better?

I heard they gave you a shot at the airport which made you ill.

Yes.

Do you still have a temperature?

No.

She took the child's hand and led her out. Her whispered voice trailed from the corridor. Hush. Don't touch. Don't touch. Hush.

*S*econd Katherine stood at the open doorway seeking an invitation to enter.

Are you leaving already?

Seventh Jill was cramming her belongings into the same suitcase she had used since she first left home for school at the age of fourteen. The two closets in her room were open wide as were her bureau drawers. She looked for the cufflinks she had given him for his last Christmas which he had never worn, and found the small gray velvet box in which they were kept inside the top bureau drawer. She tucked the box in a corner of the suitcase and pulled down the lid.

Well I don't actually have to leave tonight. Classes don't begin till the day after tomorrow but I decided to take an apartment instead of staying in the dormitory this term. I'd like to get there a day ahead in case of emergency.

Let me help you.

Second Katherine crossed the threshold and pushed the other end of the lid down deftly working in stray bits of clothing squeezed out of containment.

I can do it myself.

They both pushed and tugged very hard while the suitcase sank deep into the mattress. Two clicks suddenly and it was done.

Well thank you. I guess that's all. Now I'll make my last run. Gangway.

She picked up the suitcase and set it outside in the corridor. She picked up her shoe bag by the straps, slung it over one shoulder and ran out of her room to the end of the corridor and entered his room on tiptoe. She stood by the foot of his bed under the opaque glass fixture in the center of the ceiling. Under the fixture dangled a huge gray seagull shot and stuffed by Sixth Michael. The two tips of the bird's outstretched wings drooped at an angle, the bones there having been broken in transit from school to home.

Her glance took in the curtained windows, the bulge of the pillows under the russet bedspread, the lamp table to the right of the bed topped by a tall lamp which gave light while he read in bed. A string he once attached to the chain-pull to simplify switching the light on or off still dangled from under the shade. Two shoulder-high chests of drawers each decorated with leather-framed family photographs and the camphor-lined chest on the floor filled with a lifetime of worn sweaters which he would not cast out. Above the chest hung an ink scroll of groups of sages chatting under the bamboo grove or sipping tea in a pavilion overlooking a placid lake. On the farther shore a bare-legged man carried a bundle of firewood on his back facing the mountain he was about to climb.

She opened the door to his bathroom and found Third Christine on her knees, bending over the edge of the tub to bathe her babies all seven of them together in the tub.

Well good-bye alligators I have to go now. See you in the summer maybe.

She ran away from their splashings and cries, ran down the corridor and through every room of the apartment until she returned to the original point of departure, closed her bedroom door, picked up her suitcase and walked slowly down the corridor toward the hall where everyone waited to say good-bye.

*S*he crossed the barrier to the place where the luggage would arrive and gave the porter her two luggage stubs. A moment later the window at the end of the conveyor belt slid open and the first suitcases rolled jerkily along the moving belt. Her porter diligently checked out the number tags on each bag as it came his way.

The door leading to the airfield swung open. An airport official, an anxious expression on his face, entered bearing a canvas suitcase the zipper of which had come undone. Bits of its contents stuck out under the open flap. He carried the suitcase across his extended arms as if it were a platter heaped with food for a banquet.

She wondered whether her two bags had weathered the journey, especially the one containing the gifts. The porter found her two bags, lugged them onto his cart and wheeled them out to a line of waiting taxis. She entered the car and gave the driver her address, adding that she hoped the trip to the city would not take long as she had an appointment at noon.

It was just twenty after eleven as the car turned into the highway. At five minutes before noon the driver stopped in front of her building. She paid him, looked up and down the Avenue then carried her suitcases into the courtyard.

She unlocked the door of her apartment, stooped to pick up the pile of mail just inside and placed it on the hall table. She brought her suitcases inside and closed the door. Then she went into the bedroom, picked up the telephone, called his office and was told he was not there.

She rolled up the window blinds in the two front rooms, opened the window of the kitchen and the bathroom, stripped to her slip and took off her stockings which a moment later she regretted having done for perhaps she should go downstairs to check with the house guardian if anyone had come earlier to look for her. She carried her suitcases into the bedroom, undid the locks and dumped the contents on the floor by the closet to sort out later after having taken a bath.

The doorbell rang twice. She rushed to the door in her bare feet and standing on tiptoe drew back the bolt. He was already pushing at the door from the other side as she drew the second bolt. Without a word they hugged and kissed. He shut the door and held her tightly. She caressed his shoulders and the back of his neck and noticed that he had lost weight. Finally she said how happy she was to see him though she still had not really had a chance to look at him because he was kissing her hair. Almost missed him she continued bending her head back so that she could finally look at him just arrived truly not more than five minutes and if he had come ten minutes ago they would have missed each other. They hugged and kissed and she said how dirty she was she hadn't even brushed her teeth. She chatted breathlessly and touched him and smiled and chatted and laughed. He remained silent, eyes avoiding hers as if listening for another voice but continued to kiss her softly all over her face alternately holding her tight then letting her go. They separated and came together, separated and came together from room to room and each time she had more to add about her trip, breathless inconsequential sentences, phrases incomplete, exclamations, but always with reference to him how she had missed him while doing this and that. She had wondered if he had remained in town during all these weeks she had kept up with news from his city read that the weather had been hideously cold the worst winter in one hundred years. Yes he still had a cold and a sore throat and she had walked and walked and walked to find him a rose-colored sweater which he had once told her he wanted and she thought that she could surely find it in her own city she had almost made the trip really to find and return with a rose-colored sweater, wait, not true he said and she broke away from him, opened her closet and pulled out a multicolored blouse of pinks reds oranges and fuchsias, Define rose. Rose is rose. No she wanted him to show her which is rose. She held up the blouse for his inspection. He pointed to a pale pink which certainly was not the color of the sweater she had finally bought one in a raspberry hue but she had some shirts which weren't really too bad she had spent so much time looking.

While she brushed her teeth at the sink, he hovered close by her in the doorway and stroked her back. What did she have on her back, she said what, buttons he said. Then she must take a bath. He said yes take a bath. She turned on the taps, rinsed out the grit accumulated at the bottom and measured a capful of jelly-like pine and hazelnut concoction which she held under the running water. Ah the same old foam he said. When she pulled up the handle to flush the toilet it was he who remembered that the handle had to be pressed down in order for the tank to refill.

Had he written much she said getting into the tub. No he hadn't written at all he had forgotten how to write. But what about all those articles she had read in his newspaper while she was away. She used to rush downtown every Thursday to a bookshop specializing in foreign periodicals to buy his newspaper well then who

wrote all that stuff. A black man. What? A little black
man. Oh he meant a ghost writer? Exactly. Did she
know that in his country a lot of people were still analphabetic. Did he mean peasants and so forth who didn't
know how to read or write? Yes he had become analphabetic while she was away. She quoted him passages
from one of his recent articles in which he stated that
it was not possible to make a film about workers because they were anti-personages and actors who attempted to portray workers ended up by aping them in
imitating their inability to make liaisons between words.
And while he was intellectually and emotionally inclined toward the worker the values of the worker he
nonetheless was unable to shed his middle-class background had always looked straight into eyes of chiefs of
enterprises but that his glance would waver when con-
fronting that of a worker so that even if he had become
analphabetic during her absence she was pleased to note
that he was now capable of effecting his liaisons properly . . .

He lurched from the seat of the covered toilet,
swooped down on her in the tub and pinched her in the
stomach. How dared she make fun of him.

Talk to her she had lost the habit of speaking his
language this last effort exhausted her. Besides she
didn't want to do all the talking. All right then while
she was away would she believe that he would find himself on the street looking up at her windows with drawn
blinds. And even when he saw that he would take the
elevator to her floor and stand outside her door and ring

and ring the doorbell. He paused. Was it really true? The second pause lasted longer. No not really true. When she stepped out of the tub he helped her dry.

They both stared at the bed. Everything is so dusty she smoothed the blanket with her hand it was so dusty. Not dusty inside he pulled off the blanket. She got in at the right he got in at the left and they quietly held each other for a time without either moving. Then he started to kiss her. He unbuttoned her robe, raised her body slightly and took off the robe. She closed her eyes as he moved and she felt his weight along the length of her. How she loved him how she thought of him every day and she kissed him all over his face and caressed his hair and his body.

It was dark when he had to go and he ought to let her sleep because she hadn't slept the night before. Where was he going, would he return later? He had an appointment at the office. After that he had to go to the hospital. Why did he have to go to the hospital? To visit someone he could be back in town by nine and he would take her out to eat something because she had nothing in the house. Or else if she preferred he could bring her something to eat. Wouldn't it be too late for him? What time did he have to be home? Tonight he didn't have to return because his wife was away. Where had she gone? She was in hospital. Was she ill? No she had had a baby. Was he happy to have the child? For him it was a bother but women want to have children.

*A*mah appeared in the shadow of the doorway to watch.

I am running out of paper bags.

Amah disappeared into the laundry room through the connecting door of the two corridors and returned immediately with several empty paper cartons which she deposited on the floor beside the bulging bags.

Seventh Jill's room appeared smaller than she had remembered it although it had been years she had not seen it but now that she had returned it was to be her retreat. She was surprised to find no one had removed baby clothes hanging limply on baby hangers with dangling strips of fabric sewn halfway down the middle of the side seams, bands which amah tied together into crisp voluptuous bows behind Seventh Jill's little back, those gathered little sleeves still puffed which amah spent interminable hours to iron, her pride, just right. She slipped the dresses from their hangers and stuffed them into brown paper bags lying on the floor. Into the bags also went the contents of three drawers of the bureau standing between the bathroom and the closet doors with mirrored panes. She did not put away the hangers but left them on the rods to use later to hang up her own clothers.

In the bottom drawer of the chest she found hidden under folds of white cotton underwear soft from years of faithful and thorough laundering and bleaching, made softer by the years, a tarnished silver porringer with an ornate handle. Although she put away the underwear into the paper bags she kept the porringer with the intention of asking amah for it. If amah were to refuse should she risk the refusal or hide it and keep it without permission?

Dyadya stood alone in the same shadowy doorway dressed in a pair of shabby trousers decades old and a pair of old camel hair slippers. Over his shirt he wore a woolen cardigan she had begun knitting for him in return for the typewriter he had brought to her at school. When she had finished knitting it, it was too small. She had unraveled and rewound and reknitted it stitch by stitch and she could not remember his ever wearing it until now the seventh consecutive day since Seventh Jill fell asleep in one of the two beds close to the window in the room that used to be occupied by First Nancy and Second Katherine. The venetian blinds were drawn. Each slat closed tightly one over the other. Moved by wind which entered the half-open window the blinds tapped gently at the glass window shield. Through the space not covered by the blind, she saw tender piercing green of new trees and golden meadows. Where Seventh Jill slept still as death, all was obscure except for a shaft of light which lit up the radiator cover that was level with the windowsill.

She needs sleep. But she had been sleeping for seven days.

He shook his head, his face sharp with anxiety.

Seventh Jill's belongings had been packed away. The bags and cartons had disappeared from the floor. Her own dresses were now hanging on miniature hangers in the two closets and her clothes rested in the three drawers. In a back corner of the bottom drawer she had hidden the silver porringer.

The inspector toured the premises of the gigantic hydroelectric complex of which Seventh Jill's room, now her own, was a part hidden behind an unfrequented recess of cavernous spaces defined by walls girded with pipes and bristling with immense wheels, a vast network of turbines and engines crossed by iron bridges and stairways. Metal beams overhead crisscrossed above huge twisting ducts. The power had been turned off.

He entered her dwarf hideaway sat on the edge of her bed while she stood at the end of the room by the two windows sealed from air and dirt. She looked longingly at the park outside spread with blossoming trees. She waited for his question.

What are your aspirations?

She knew the answer but could not remember it. He turned to leave. She grabbed his hat to keep a part of him, to establish a link, a pretext for a later meeting when she might be able to give him the answer.

Dyadya appeared at the doorway, his face frowning with disapproval on seeing her with the hat. She pretended to be a clown and danced a vivacious jig a clown's dance tossing the hat repeatedly in the air then catching it until he left in puzzlement.

In that instant of silence after his departure the answer came to her. The hat clutched tightly in both hands her only passport she dashed out of the room to overtake him. She raced through passageways along the iron bridges ran up ran down her steps echoing. At last she came to a door which surprisingly opened at the first twist of the handle and she found herself outdoors gasping in the cold air her breath formed vaporous puffs, her heart pounded.

The gray horizon merged with the cloudless sky. Around her were snow-covered plains. She saw a track in the snow and followed it around the dark looming edifice. She heard engines starting up and men's voices. She turned a corner and with relief saw a figure seated at the wheel of a tractor. The engine started.

Wait. Wait for me.

He cut his engine. She ran up to him an old wrinkled man.

I cannot. I am late as it is. They have gone ahead of me.

Wait. Return this to him.

The old man nodded, accepted the hat which he put on the ledge beside his seat. He started the engine. Slowly the machine rumbled off.

She heard someone crying in the dark and reached up to turn on the light. Tears were streaming down her cheeks.

*S*he woke up and got out of bed to sort out the pile of belongings which she had dumped on the floor. Without bothering to hang up her clothes she found enough space in the cupboard shelves to cram in everything that she picked off the floor. She felt driven to clear the disorder of the bedroom. She would rearrange later.

The doorbell rang. Once again he was pushing at the other side of the door while she was still turning the bolt back. He gave her a perfunctory kiss when he entered and made straight for the kitchen where he poured himself a glass of water from the tap. He could not stay for the night. He went into the bedroom to telephone.

She got back into the unmade bed and drew the covers up to her ears. While holding the telephone to his ear with one hand his other brushed at something on the sheet next to her pillow. She wanted to touch him but drew back her hand. He saw the movement, reached out and held her hand until he had finished talking on the telephone.

She was soaking in her bed. The oilcloth under the sheet was crumpled and out of place. She felt hot and cold. She got up and was astonished by her body's weightlessness. She opened the door and wandered out into the empty corridor. Holding on to the wall to keep herself steady, the cold stone underfoot soothed and consoled her. She came to a door above which shone a soft diffused red light. She opened the door and stepped out on a staircase of open metal grillwork open to the sky she could see the stars. She heard amah's voice behind her.

What are you doing here? You'll catch a terrible cold. This is no time to take a walk. Go back to bed.

Amah led her back to the room, turned on a green shaded bedside lamp and exclaimed when she pulled away the top sheet, uncovering the pool of blood. She hastily stripped the bed and removed the blot.

Have I lost him? Is it all over?

She got back into bed. Shivering between clean icy sheets she heard him wade out of water.

Marry me.

She half turned her head on the pillow, squinting her eyes against the light of the lamp shining in her face. Amah leaned out of the darkness and fed her a spoonful of medicine from a bottle on the lamp table. Amah turned out the light.

Marry me.

Why?

Because I love you.

Because of the baby?

Marry me and have the baby. Don't go away.

It is over. She cried in the dark, remembering sunlight and water, her face pressed against the rock.

He replaced the telephone and leaned back so that his head rested on her stomach, his face turned away from her. She stroked his hair in slow lingering motions, stroking another.

Shouldn't you go now?

The doctor is on his way. He'll call me around midnight.

She continued to stroke his hair except for an instant when she felt a sudden soreness bite into her side that was under the weight of his head. She shifted her body slightly. He raised his head.

I'm leaving now.

She got up with him and went into the kitchen to pour into a glass the remains of a bottle of white wine opened before her departure. When she returned to the living room he had his coat on.

Don't you want to take these with you as long as you

are going home? She picked up a shirt on the living room couch.

I'll take them another time. It's not so amusing now.

Better take them now. I have no place to keep them. I am sorry I wasn't successful in finding you a pink sweater. This blue shirt is rather nice though. You'll need a bag, let me see . . .

This will do.

He picked up a large paper shopping bag lying under the table.

But there is a hole in it.

Doesn't matter.

She covered the hole with tissue paper and placed the sweater and shirts, folded, in the bag and added more tissue paper on the top. At the door he turned around as if he had forgotten something. He dropped the bag on the floor, took out his appointment book from an inner pocket of the coat and headed toward the doorway of the kitchen. She had not expected this kindness from him. He turned the pages while muttering.

Let's see now. Can't see you on Monday. Too many appointments. Tuesday's my day at the hairdresser I spend almost the entire day there. Wednesday I have to work and Thursday too. Friday. We can see each other on Friday. I'll telephone you Friday.

He made a note on the page.

Yes.

He kissed her on the forehead before picking up the bag. She opened the door. There was no light in the corridor.

Let me put on the light.

No. Don't bother.

He strode to the elevator and waited. She pushed the light button outside her door, flooding the corridor in orange light. He looked at her, a great big grin, quite idiotic, spread over his face. She waved good-bye as he stepped into the elevator, the grin still on his face.

I have given my party and now must clean thoroughly to make order in my room. Amah has already gone to bed so I shall shut the door between her quarters and the laundry room.

How soothing the sound of running water. While I watch the water rising gradually in the sink, I add a bit of detergent with a slight shake of the box so that not too much spills out. No waste. The time I used to spend crushing wisteria pods to make soap to wash laundry along the banks of the canal.

Wet four cheesecloth towels in the water. Wring them out. I need four damp cheesecloth towels to clean my room.

There is a science to thorough housecleaning and no one knows better than I how to go about it. First prepare the room for cleaning. Remove from the room anything that does not belong in it such as cigarette butts in ashtrays, newspapers, strings, paper wrappings, half-empty glasses, bottles and crumpled napkins. Then put away anything that belongs in the room but is out of place such as this book which belongs on the fourth shelf to the left of the fireplace. Now the field is clear and I can begin.

I raise the blinds as high as they can go. Then I climb on to the window ledge. You see I do not start in any old way. My system is to start from the heights and work toward the base. Start with the big and end with the small. From the end to the beginning. Dust that falls from the heights can be wiped up later while dust that falls after the lower areas have been cleaned means one would have to start cleaning all over again.

I wipe the windowpanes from top to bottom with a surface of damp cheesecloth which becomes smaller and contracts as I continuously fold in the dirt so that each pane has the benefit of being wiped with a fresh surface of the towel. Now I take another towel which has not yet been used and apply myself to cleaning the woodwork between the glass panes and the window frame, taking good care not to miss the dirt in corners and cracks. Dirt does not escape my eye.

It is late. The light from my room outlines my figure balanced on the window ledge. There are no lights in the buildings across the street. The street lights are on, a straight line of lights going far into the distance, the direction we always take driving to the country. Little by little I lower the blinds, very slowly so that I can wipe the outer side and the inner side in one operation. I crouch lower and lower as the blinds descend until I find it more convenient to get off the ledge and stand on the floor to clean the lower areas of the blind. I have now used up four towels which I shall rinse out in the laundry room sink that is filled with water and detergent.

The water darkens as I rinse out the dirt from the four cheesecloths. I squeeze them dry and let the dark water flow out, splashing the ebbing water against the sides of the sink so that no rings of dirt cling. I refill with fresh water, add about the same amount of detergent sparingly and am now prepared to resume the next round in the cleaning of my room.

For the next stage I shall need the ladder. I untwist the cheesecloths and drape them over a rung of the aluminum stepladder thus leaving my hands free to carry the ladder into my room where I deposit it in front of the fireplace that is underneath the bamboo-framed ideogram depicting my emblem embroidered on pink silk in multicolored hues of pinks, reds and browns and greens. I climb the ladder with towel in hand and gently pull forward the bamboo frame. With one firm wipe the top is clean. This I do also on the two sides and the bottom, always folding the towel, thus folding in the dirt after each wipe. I have one clean surface left. I wipe the glass protecting my emblem and rearrange the frame so that it hangs centered and in line with the fireplace mantel.

I bring the ladder to the other side of the room and place it, after pulling the bamboo couch away from the wall where three embroidered panels in varying arrangements of birds beasts trees and flowers hang framed in ebony-encrusted blossoms of mother-of-pearl. I also shift the two lamp bases of bronze herons with wings folded and beaks upturned which flank the bamboo and silk cushioned couch. You ask why I leave the fireplace area which I have not yet completed cleaning to come to this side of the room. It is because I follow the system of starting high, finishing low.

I place the ladder between the wall and the back of the couch. I climb up the ladder and take a clean damp cloth and pulling the frame gently forward I wipe around each of the three panels in the same way I wiped my emblem above the fireplace.

Now the glass shelves from floor to ceiling on the wall opposite the windows pose problems. I must remove the objects from each shelf before wiping the shelf clean. There are two alternatives. I can remove all the objects from all the shelves, wipe the shelves in one sweep then replace the objects shelf by shelf after having wiped each object. That will mean several trips up and down the ladder, without taking into account the walking one would do in carrying the objects to the heavy glass coffee table in the center of the room. Or else I can transfer the objects on the top shelf to the shelf below, wipe the top shelf then replace the objects after cleaning each one thoroughly thus progressing downward, shelf by shelf. I choose to do the latter.

I stand on the top rung of the ladder and pick up the pink bird cage with the bluebird inside and deposit that on the shelf below. I wipe the shelf then the bird cage not forgetting to give the bottom a wipe in case it has picked up any dust from resting on the unwiped surface of the shelf immediately below. The top shelf done. Now for the next. I pick up the accordion pleated miniature panels of still lives painted with colors of genuine vegetable floral and powdered stone dyes. I wipe the shelf. I pick up the panels and holding them at arm's length I turn from the shelves and I lightly blow away the dust that might have collected on the fragile surfaces. I turned away so as not to blow back any dust on the shelves already wiped. I follow this procedure until I reach the shelf that is midway between the ceiling and the floor. At this point I step down and carry the ladder out into the hall, having no further use for it. Otherwise the pattern is the same. However on the bottom shelf where some books are stacked I do not displace them but wipe the exposed part of the shelf then wipe the books even though the moisture from the cloth might eventually tatter the bindings but my way is effective in removing the dust.

When that is finished I go out into the hall pick up the ladder and carry it together with my soiled towels into the laundry room. I set the ladder against the wall and rinse the cloths which turns the water dark. I listen to the sound of dripping water. Amah sleeps quietly in her quarters inside the room where his things are stored. I wring out the towels, empty and refill the sink as before and return to my room to continue to clean and make order.

The mantel is crowded with offerings. There is a carved miniature table of teak and ebony and rosewood on top of which rests a miniature silver melon with stem leaves and vines. There is a measuring tape encased in silver, a French crystal vase etched all over with vines, picture cards commemorating the yearly occasions of my life, a soapstone bust and a photograph of us standing together in the vegetable plot, his arm around my waist that has thickened over the years. We are both dressed in trousers and look very tall. At the very end of the mantel stands a box of decorative matches. The fireplace below is empty, has never been used and therefore collects no dust.

I have cleaned the writing desk, the glass coffee table with its centerpiece of heavy stoneware dish enameled with life-sized purple irises. There is no use taking out the vacuum cleaner to clean the small oval carpet under the coffee table. I can clean it better and faster by going down on my hands and knees and wiping clean the tufts with my damp cloths. I mop the parquet around it not with a dry but with a damp mop which picks up more dust than dry. I push back the bamboo couch against the wall, move the herons back into place, rinse out the cloths and hang them to dry, rinse out the mop turn out the light.

Now that I am alone she no longer troubles me. Tomorrow my firstborn son will come to fetch me for the drive to the country where I shall put flowers in front of his altar. She may come along if she wishes. I accept. Now I can shut the door and sleep my room is clean and in order.

*T*wenty minutes after the start of trade an opening block of 10,000 shares crossed the tape at 125, five points below the previous close and twenty points below the all-time high registered on the day when he had completed his buying the week before. Time to pause and watch.

Time now to equalize the portions of his extensions. All must be equal no one part of more value than the other. Nevertheless check buying power in each account. Every little attention brings further progress.

He dialed Margin Department on the telephone and asked for debit balances, buying power in accounts 595220, 595221, 595222, 595223, 595224, 595225, 595226, 595227.

Three transactions crossed the tape consecutively, 100 shares up a quarter, 100 shares up one half, then 400 shares price unchanged from the preceding trade. Firm so far but the day was early. He opened the top drawer of his desk and took out a batch of order slips and squared off the pile like a pack of cards and placed it against the low glass panel which rose above the front edge of his shallow desk. He pushed back his chair for a better view of the board which covered one entire wall of the room starting from the floor and stopping short several feet below the ceiling, with just enough space on the wall for the narrow horizontal screen that pictured the crossing of the ticker tape.

It came on again clipped a quarter on 100 shares followed seconds later by 200 shares at one half. Not going one way or the other, holding pretty steady so far after yesterday's drop. Still too early to tell. He reached into his bottom drawer and pulled out the individual aluminum panels on which transactions were recorded for the year, current holdings marked on cards on one side of the panel and holdings sold on the other side.

The telephone rang. He noted down some figures on his open desk calendar.

Account 595220 Margined. With enough purchasing power to buy another 500. Enough. She might need cash to cover repairs and a new paint job on the country house. If only he could get away and rest. Do some planting in the country. Another two days to go before the weekend. Two more nights staying up to attend her sorrows. Life is change, we live in change. Please I want you to accept now that she is to have our grandchild. I need some rest.

On the tape 300 shares crossed at 124, 1000 at 125. No change. Should he enter and buy just to see which way the price would go. Test it a little. A sharp pain pressed into his side and he took out the bottle from his desk and shook out two pills which he swallowed dry before recapping the bottle. He sat back and watched the tape for the next price.

In her last month he went to visit her while James was at work in the afternoon. She addressed him as Dyadya and why not? No matter what the past she was now a member of the family, she was to bear James's son. Another life, another promise. Dyadya she greeted him at the doorway. Dyadya she had just returned from a visit to the Welfare Department. What a long trip by subway to find out what items those people considered essential for a newborn baby. They certainly would be relied upon to tell the truth, not like at that department store where they tried to talk her into spending a fortune Dyadya will you believe it for all kinds of frivolities. She was determined to maintain a stringent budget. He had felt a lump in his throat. Upset and anxious he asked if she and James had enough money. If you don't have enough, please ask me.

He would leave early to buy her a gift. Something

really worthwhile. Ask for advice at home this evening. He shook his head ruefully, astonished with the force of habit. That was a mistake. Tell absolutely no one of course. He picked up the rest of the panels from the desk.

Account 595221 We traveled on the train for more than a fortnight. Ngmah was in hospital waiting for a birth and could not make the journey. The telegram arrived in the middle of my studies. Since it was a question of my mother who would not allow anyone else to operate it was unthinkable that I should not return to do her bidding.

Though she had barely begun to talk I brought her back for the brief stay, knowing that they would be glad to see her after more than a year's absence and that she would be no trouble on the journey, being a solemn and wise child and obedient. Never cried or smiled though she was not more than three at the time. We chugged along across two continents with brief stops daily at some forlorn outposts along the way for nourishment.

Later after the others arrived I told her you are my eldest, my first, you must lead and she accepted this and did the best she could and carried on for years, my deputy among her sisters, brothers and strangers. I took it for granted and perhaps this was too much of a strain. After the accident I visited her in her room. Her face was covered with bandages. I could only see her eyes and her mouth. We sat side by side on the couch and I held her hand without speaking. We both looked at the opposite wall as if still on the train looking at the mournful passing landscape. Everything is all right. You have done your duty, there is no need to do more. I love you because you are mine.

When we arrived she did not talk not knowing the language. After the operation we took the journey back. We talked. Sometimes I fed her nursed her and we kept each other company. In our closeness we were silent most of the time and looked at the landscape moving past our window.

Account 595222 When she finally came home after spending three years in the tropics I waited at the gate and watched the plane come down. It was my mistake not to have heeded her hesitations. I urged her instead to go persuading her that it was for her own good. Now she is returning alone without him but carrying his child. She was not tough enough to stand the wilderness.

They let me pass through the grilled metal door even before the plane halted on the runway. She was the last passenger to come out. I saw her maneuver each step with caution, her hands clinging onto the rails, the child in her barely concealed under the long coat I had bought her as a farewell present wishing her happiness and my blessings. My throat contracted at the sight of her and I started running toward her as she was halfway down. I ran and ran to take back that portion of me that I had once so thoughtlessly relinquished and caught her in my arms before her foot set on ground. I love her because she is mine.

Account 595223 She wants nothing. She produces life. Completely out of the running in this system of balances and counterbalances I have devised over the years to maintain harmony and equilibrium between the head and my extensions and the extensions among themselves. She plays her primal biological role, bearing one child after another and with fierce stubbornness wards off life's decorations and pretensions unafflicted and disregarding ambition not related to the producing and caring of children, withdrawing to an out of the way hole in the world like a rabbit burrowed in a dark tunnel. She does not add to me nor take away, she makes no demands. She is content. I love her because she is mine. For the content and repose she gives me.

Account 595224 Between her wanting and not wanting she left me in constant confusion at each of our encounters. She took rage and order from me and still it seemed insufficient she was incomplete cold and hungry. Now that she is about to leave I must tell her that during these years she should not have minded if I could not always express it because it was not in my nature and my habit to express it so often. Yet in this country it is done and I am learning, but I am always there for her for all my children and I love her. So all she needs in life other than what she already has from me and my love is hope and courage. Hope and courage. And I will back her up. And I cupped her face in the palm of my hands, looked into her eyes and smiled. I am your Father and I love you because you are mine. Hope and courage.

Account 595225 I waited for him a long time. When finally he came I found him so unlike me. His lack of

emotion relieved me from the burden of mine and re-
assured me that he would be counted on to do the right
thing. I waited for him a long time. When he came
recognition was automatic. I did not question him he
was my firstborn son. Neither did he seem to question
his position so I never asked him if he knew his role.
Since he never spoke I was convinced we were in accord.
I was therefore taken by surprise and at first blamed
him for not being willing to play out my expectations.
And I began a crash program of lectures to correct our
misunderstanding. I was much disappointed and ex-
cluded him for many years. Now that he has come to
me for help I cannot refuse him my firstborn son and
I love him because he is mine. I waited for him a long
time.

Account 595226 We raced on the cement walk by
the edge of the river. Catch me if you can I shouted
playing the game with him whenever we took our walks
by the river. Can you catch me? That day he gained
upon me and without stopping to tag me ran ahead to
the end of the cement walk. He took me by surprise. I
considered the event a flash in the pan. I forgot about
the race and continued to question him relentlessly, fear-
ing that he would be a dropout from the mainstream of
his duties since he spent so much time hunting and fishing, singing and strumming his guitar. Once he wrecked
a car and I felt myself jeopardized by his existence and
his actions he was so much a part of me. I walked in
the garden, the garden rake was balanced over my
shoulder. He followed behind while I questioned him.

In order to make a point clear because I was not sure if he understood I turned and my rake struck him on the forehead. He was hurt but I felt his hurt was mine and I was furious that he had placed my life in jeopardy by not watching where he was going. I love him because he is mine. I did not think we could have made it but together we did.

Account 595227 We went out to the country to water the potted plants that had been brought indoors at the start of winter. Normally during winter we would drive out every two weeks not only to water the plants but also to check the oil and the pipes, but due to a heavy snowfall and below freezing temperatures immediately after we put off going for three weeks.

I stopped the car at the foot of the driveway and we told her to stay in the car until our return. I turned off the headlights and shut the door of the car. Although dusk had settled we could still see our way to the house by the light of the snow. It took us a while to get there because of the deep snow and frozen crust above. We watered the plants and checked the oil and pipes. There were traces of mice in the kitchen so we also laid poison in corners under the sink and behind the refrigerators and also in the cupboards where we kept food staples such as boxes of rice and canned goods. Then we turned out the lights and locked the back door after having checked all the other doors which gave out to the garden. It was darker than before and we decided to take a shortcut across the garden to the car rather than follow the driveway along which we had originally come. We trudged slowly and with much difficulty side by side knee-deep through the snow. We could barely make out the shape of our car parked at the foot of the driveway.

Someone moved along the driveway toward the house. The figure stopped. After a second it moved away from the driveway toward the open fields lost balance and fell in the snow. We stopped and called out. The figure got up from the snow and made a few awkward steps toward us. We all came together by the car. What happened? Where were you going? She said she had been frightened by the length of our absence, had left the car in search of us. We looked like two bears crossing the garden. She had panicked and had run into the fields. She had expected us to return by the same way. The bears were out to get her.

We all got into the car and I driving home with her in the back seat was haunted by the expression of relief on her wet child face when we rejoined her by the car. She slept in the back of the car all the way home. The last born is loved like all the rest but a little more.

*T*he meeting was held in an oak paneled room with deep blue carpets wall to wall in the tower of a skyscraper. The window of the room overlooked the entrance of the harbor.

They sat around a polished oak table and the manager read out the terms of the bid. She looked out the window at the piers and boats in the harbor, then looked at the gigantic overhanging cloud in which she saw plains, mountains, forests, rivers, deserts, chasms, a whole continent reflected. Meetings were held every day in all sorts of rooms to arrange financing for construction of bridges, canals, housing, highways, waterworks, power works, sewage, ports, terminals that developed the potential of the land and harnessed its forces through unending cycles of debt and repayment.

The manager asked each man if his firm chose to go along with the terms or wanted out. Each man simply replied yes or no or whether they wanted more participation. Then the meeting ended.

It was the first of such meetings she attended. Astonished, then exhilarated, at the brevity and matter of fact financial ways of implementing monumental public works projects, she asked her companion who daily attended such sessions Is that all, do you mean that's all there is to it? as they hurried back to the office through the dark afternoon crowds.

Just about. The managing firm puts in the bid and we wait for the result, hopeful of course that our group will win.

And if we lose?

We'll try for another issue.

She wanted to talk to him, to see him, and hurried down the corridor toward the board room afraid that he might have already left for the day though it was scarcely a quarter of an hour since the close of market. He was apt to leave early these days.

She saw him seated in his usual place as she neared the glass wall. Approaching from behind him, she noiselessly slid into a chair beside him, grateful and relieved to find him still there. She looked up at the board, then looked at him. Today she could not tell. Quite often she could by a mere glance at the posture of his body, the way he sat in his chair, the angle of his head, gauge the tempo and condition of the day's market.

How was the market today?

Very active. I did a lot of work today. Exhausted.

She kept silent while he studied the figures on the board, columns of names of companies, prices of the day, first, high, low, last, now immobile and silent, but which buzzed and clicked out the changes all through the trading hours from ten to three-thirty.

The narrow horizontal screen above the board was blank, the light switched off till the start of trade next day when symbols and numbers again would glide across the edge right to left like ships sailing in and out of view across a harbor.

Time to go home.

Without taking his glance off the board he began to tidy up his desk, tearing and crumpling incompleted order slips and dropping them in the wastebasket under his desk. He threw out a pile of printed reports into the basket then tore off and crumpled the scribbled top page of his desk calendar and stuffed papers into his soft leather portfolio which he then zipped closed. In a final gesture he swept stray pencils, ballpoint pens and clips into the top drawer of his desk, closed the drawer and got to his feet.

What did you do today?

I went to my first municipal bond pricing.

Very good. Did you learn anything?

Yes.

He patted her arm and smiled.

Soon I shall be learning from you. You will give me lessons.

He laughed and nudged her again as he walked slowly to the coat closet.

Oh stop it Dyadya.

She laughed too and followed him.

Are you going home now?

He did not seem to have heard as he took his coat off the hanger.

No rest. One's got to keep on top of situations in constant flux and change. No rest. I'm stopping by to say hello to Second Katherine.

She held his leather portfolio while he pushed his left arm into the coat sleeve. Then she helped him get into the right as he had an ache in that shoulder. She straightened and smoothed down his coat collar.

I'll take a walk with you to the elevator.

Very good.

They walked in silence through the empty corridor and into the empty reception room. He pushed open one of the two thick plate glass doors and she followed him out to the elevators.

A bell rang, a button flashed red and the double doors slid open.

With a brief nod toward her he took his leave.

See you tomorrow Dyadya.

Just before the doors slid shut she rushed forward to

hand him his leather portfolio which she had almost forgotten.

Everyone had left for the day. She sat at her desk. Half an hour to spare before the beginning of her accounting class, about a five minute walk from the office. In the hollow silence a telephone rang twice somewhere in the offices, then stopped. The light snapped on in the Telex machine beside her desk. All at once the automatic keys of the machine started chopping away, feeding out lines of news, the results of a West Coast bidding. Water power construction on the Missouri River. The name of the city was unknown to her and she picked up the map book from a nearby desk to pinpoint the location.

She turned the pages to Missouri and found the river, then turned more pages to find the source. Entranced by its length, the river flowed through seven states, she traced the course of the water, her lips moved in silence and wonder, linking names of colors beasts saints trees ideas Indians rocks the names of men, a holy procession signifying man's enduring tenure.

*O*n her terrace the apple tree made a red-leafed ball supported by a slender purple trunk. Miniature leaves shimmered off gold and silver sparks at the wind's coming. A craze of blossoms arrived one morning, the tree's first flowering on her terrace.

They had chosen it together one windless day the first spring sunlit day of the year from an assortment spread out in rows in open fields burlap tied and root bundled trees stacked and ranged in lengthy rows for inspection.

All shapes of trunks and branches and still leafless under blue skies clung with wispy white streaks.

We are going to get another tree for your terrace. I am coming to fetch you.

I cannot have another tree. I've made arrangements to leave.

No you'll stay and marry me.

She left the door open but he rang the bell anyway before entering and stood just inside against the closed door to contemplate the shapes and colors of objects and space from a reverent devotional distance.

I love you and all objects here alive with you. Shades and shadows are all a part of you.

She stood in the center of the square carpet of faded reds greens and blues and whites in which she discerned oases and deserts, scorpions and camels, departures, wanderings and homecomings woven inextricably there.

What do you see?

He paced into the room stopping short at the carpet border.

A garden enclosed by four white walls. In one corner a low hugging couch topped by two enormous pillows covered by an indeterminate yellow stuff of canvas silk or suede. A square table of carved ebony, the four sides stiff with twining vines beasts and flowers. On the wall hang tributes of flowers in shapes of flowers, squares, circles and triangles. They are painted in a multitude of colors lavender, pink, greige, beige, orange and lemon. Perched on a horizontal branch centered against a black moon a full-throated thrush stuffed and unruffled points its beak toward blood behind thorns dripping down the face of a man hanging limp on the tree. A landscape in winter. The flowing calligraphy above explicates the artist's excellence in portraying a bare branched tree in a freeze as solid and deep as the rocks upon which it roots. Three white boxes measured to the height of your head. Behind their doors lie hidden linens, pillows, quilts, silks, scarves, ribbons, stones and gold, your beggar's repository, storeroom of visibles and invisibles of your life don't leave me.

They drove through canyoned streets washed clean by spring rain that made the heart leap, past empty doorways, lettered storefronts set above sheets of dark window glass. No sign of life this early hour of Sunday morning. Under the musty gloom of an arch of grates and girders which led to the approach of the ramp they paused for the light to change. The car mounted a curved ramp. All at once they gained the sunbathed high road which ran along the edge of the broad river.

They crossed the bridge and drove through marshland landscape. Miles of shallow canals and freight tracks cut patterns in the russet marsh grass. On the tip of a gigantic derrick a hallucinatory flame ball danced in frenzy.

They returned when the sun dropped burning on the edge of the sulfurous sky. In the shadow of her building he freed the tree imprisoned in the trunk of the car, a swaying willow shivering and leafless.

He carried it out to the terrace and in the last light

planted it in the red fir box into which he first poured a sack of soil. With his bare hands he scooped a hollow in the center, unwrapped the burlap from the hardened earth caked around the roots and swung stem and root into the hollow. She steadied the tree while he emptied another sack of soil till the earth was level with the box edge. He pressed the soil firmly around the stem then smoothed it over. She fetched a jug of water which he poured in slow circular motions around the tree. They watched the water soak and disappear slowly into the soil.

*I*n the morning when she arrived the telephone on her desk rang before she had time to take off her coat. We're lunching at twelve, and he had hung up before she had had time to reply. Knowing him sure enough he couldn't hold down the pressure. Nevertheless she had not expected him to have it out with her so soon in the day. He must have been brooding and building up his rancor since last night's farewell dinner during which he waited for them to come, though never mentioning their names once, still waited while she served coffee, and waited silent and reproachful when everyone said good-bye at the door.

Ten minutes before noon he appeared at the doorway of her room with his hat and raincoat clutched between arm and chest. He could not wait for her but made an abrupt motion, an angry jerk of the head to signify that she was to come instantly. She opened a drawer to put away the pens and pencils scattered about her desk and came upon the black suede jewel box containing the gold and turquoise brooch in the shape of a pineapple. I want you to have this he said handing her the box as he came up to her desk to say good-bye at the end of the afternoon. When she pulled back the lid, he smiled broadly and whispered The pineapple is the traditional symbol of hospitality. For your party tonight and because you're going away, my farewell gift.

Beautiful Dyadya but I'm not sure it's my color. It might be perfect for someone else.

You must keep it, I bought it for you. Try it on and see, you won't regret it. You can always exchange it for something else, but once you've put it on, you'll want to keep it. Keep it. Especially right for the family gathering tonight. Wear it. A gift for your hospitality.

Wondering whether to tell him, she was almost on the verge of blurting out the truth when he relieved her of the box, unclasped the brooch from its black velvet cushion and eager and awkward managed to pin it to the lapel of her suit jacket.

How well it looks on you! And I am so looking forward to tonight's dinner. Keep it.

Would it have been simpler to have told him out-right that she had not invited them. And how would she have put it. But he had not even bothered to inquire. A sense of tact perhaps or more likely an abundant confidence that she would not fail him by not asking them to the dinner, the picture having changed, their baby, the new element. The gift of the pineapple, and in much the same way his reluctant agreement to let her go away for a year, served as payment for her cooperation with his larger wishes.

Feeling vaguely resentful she closed her drawer on the box, got up and stepped quietly past rows of desks occupied by seated figures hunched over work.

He had gone past the hall. She struggled into her coat while on the run to catch up with him and found him by the elevator trying to put on his coat. When she reached over to help him he shook off her hand.

They stood facing the closed doors of the elevator without apparent notice of each other. She saw the tension in his body, his arms and elbows thrust out taut as a bow, the clenched fists. She hoped his rage would not erupt until they were clear of the building and out on the streets.

With a faint ring the double doors of the elevator slid open. She stepped in after him, relieved to see that they were not alone in the elevator.

In his single minded concentration of preparing what he would say to her and almost oblivious of her in his gathering rage, he walked ahead and pushed through the revolving doors without a glance back. He walked

ahead, crossed alone at the narrow intersection of the
street and finally paused to look back on the farther
pavement that was shaded from the bright noon sun by
the massive wall of the Sub-Treasury. The sun shone in
her eyes, she could not see him clearly through dust
particles dancing in the stiff wind and shining like gold.
Three blasts of a ship's horn came from the river. A car
stopped short to let her cross. When she stepped up the
pavement and approached him, he abruptly turned on
his heels and she followed on tiptoe in order not to
catch her heels in the open grillwork embedded in the
pavement along half the length of the street.

Once she managed to catch up to him but he quick-
ened his pace and dodged ahead. From then on he main-
tained a pace which made no allowance for her to catch
up on account of the narrow street and noontime
crowds streaming counter to her direction.

She kept track of his figure always half a block ahead
and she followed him doggedly all the way to the door
of the building which housed the restaurant. He pushed
the door and entered. She pushed it also as it was about
to swing shut in her face and followed him down a
flight of marble steps, a shortcut they often made use of
to reach the restaurant located below pavement level.
She lost him for an instant around the bend of a corridor
dimly lit by electric candelabra fixed to the walls. Just
before entering the restaurant he glanced over his shoulder to see if she was still behind him.

Unlike other days she did not accept the drink he
offered but sat with hands clasped tight against the edge

of the table while he gave the waitress their order without consulting her.

I had hoped that all my children would be generous.

She remained silent against his opening onslaught, hopeful of escape but seeing none accepted his need to vent himself.

Why do you want to go away? Why do you want to give up your work? You will have forgotten everything you learned by the time you return.

Relieved by this postponement of the central question she carefully replied in English I want to get married.

He was taken aback.

Whom do you want to marry?

I don't know.

Ridiculous. It's not true. Besides what makes you think you'll find someone when you haven't found one yet?

Might give it a try.

You're being unreasonable. Tell me truly why you want to leave. Marriage is just an excuse. You like the business I know you do, and more than that you've always wanted to do it.

I feel like doing something else for a while.

Don't be silly. What are you really going to do? You're not a serious person. I can't keep up with all your changes.

I'll be back Father. I need time to think.

Think about what? Don't you see there's no time, no time. This is a serious and hard business. You can't just leave whenever you feel like it, it's irresponsible. That's it. You are irresponsible.

If you like.

The waitress arrived, set their order on the table and moved away.

Listen to me I am your father and I know what is right for you.

Your food is getting cold Father.

He picked up a fork and abruptly laid it down.

There is no reason for you to leave and every reason for you to stay. I shall have to retire in a few years. You must stay because you have a good deal to learn. Don't assume you know it all and can come and go as you please.

He picked up the fork again. His hand trembled as he scrambled together the different foods on the plate and started to eat, digging furiously into the pile. She also picked up her fork. Suddenly he slammed down his fork on the table. It struck his plate with a clang.

I forbid you to leave. Not to recognize her is an offense to me.

It's all been arranged. I shall be gone a year. You accepted that up till last night. You already agreed to it some weeks ago. You're angry with me because they were not invited to my dinner, not because I am leaving.

I want all my children to be generous. I am disappointed with you. You have failed me. You are a failure.

He bit into his food rapidly, the hand holding the fork all the time trembling. She stopped eating and stared at her water glass.

I did not invite them last night and I do not intend to give another dinner before I go Father. That part is over. As for the other, in the beginning of our differences I believed that with time we could all get used to it, that we would eventually all accept her, that she would become a part of us, having married him. If not, we would stand to lose our unity based on the oneness of you and Ngmah which must not be shaken, under which we all submitted. I played my part in your system of balances, forever ready to forfeit what was to my own advantage so as not to shake that first principle, the essential mode and core of my existence. It was a hard lesson to come by and you required it of me. By now it has become a necessity, I hardly know how to be without it and I'm not prepared to throw it out for their sakes for their child. I want to go away. I want my separateness for a time. I don't know who I am outside of the old context and I'm afraid I might not survive the new. Besides my presence would be insupportable to you if I were not on your side.

Try it. Stay.

You're splitting the head in two. Can you sustain the injury? Ngmah is adamant. What comes after, is it worth it?

How dare you question me! I am Father I can do no wrong. In opposing me you are barbarian.

She could not contradict him, in a way she agreed with him.

You are wrong not to help me.

I wish I could. I feel a terrible danger crossing. The

oneness of you and Ngmah you have built so tightly you can't undo overnight just to accommodate them. You taught me that first hard lesson, I survived the trial and accepted my place. It's unfair to try me a second time. I can't help.

I am Father I know what is right. Wait and see. Do it for me.

I can't stand waiting around to see the old destroyed and unconvinced about the new, I waited too long too much waste to accept your order which I did for you. Now I want to go my own way.

Go. I don't want you to stay. You are not my daughter. She's the better daughter.

The waitress came to clear the table and placed a menu before each of them.

And if I were to die would you be for her? If I were to die how would you feel having opposed me?

*H*e persuaded her to come up to the island, a little rocky pine-strewn island set in the middle of still black water under vast blue skies.

He took out the canoe from its rack in the boathouse. She watched him carry the canoe, his arms raised above his head to support the two sides, his head almost hidden under the long hollow of the canoe. She stood in the middle of the gray slippery jetty partially submerged in water. Water lapping around the open spaces between the planks cooled her bare feet. She wondered if he might not slip as he sidestepped carefully down the slope balancing himself with the weight of the canoe till he reached the head of the jetty. Breathing heavily he paused. Sweat poured down his face.

He edged the boat into the water, held it steady while she climbed in and then lowered the picnic basket in the center of the canoe near her feet. He kicked off his sneakers and stepped into the canoe which bobbed violently under his weight, one side scraped against the dock till he picked up the paddle and pushed free.

She closed her eyes. The slow glide of the canoe made her slightly sick and accentuated the sensation of her body's leaden weight that living thing nestled inside of her, gliding on the black lake infinitely deep, sleep, the sun will melt the ice in the picnic basket.

The sharp crack of a gun echoed across the water from one end of the lake. She opened her eyes inquiring. He rested his paddle on the gunwale.

Afternoon race just begun. Bad day for it. No wind.

Like her, boats becalmed today, limping, sinking, no unfurling of spinnakers no haul in and release of ropes callusing hands or dodging swinging booms, no strain of scrambling, sprays in the wind. Let her sleep.

But the sky was full of hard white light which penetrated her tightly closed eyelids. The hostile water would engulf her far from the shore.

We are not moving! We are not moving!

Easy there.

Let's get back to shore we'll never reach the other side. I don't want to die in the middle of this unknown lake. Take me home. Let's go back. No picnic. Go back. We're almost there.

Reproached by his broad flat accent recalling woods and streams and outdoor things that brave the waters of the deep and look clear and stubborn into the hard white light, sees green trees and flowering fields, she lapsed into silence. He trailed his paddle in the water, watched her without expression while the canoe moved aimlessly in irregular, half-circle sweeps.

They landed on a strip, the strand end of a curl, all red rock that jutted out of the water. The inner side formed a cove which gently sloped down to a pebbled beach. On the other side facing the lake rose a sheer rock cliff. At the topmost part of the cliff was a crumbling cement and brick pile topped by two rusty metal rings once the foundation of a jumping board.

He steadied the canoe, holding it away from the pebbles until she got out with basket and paddle. Then he lifted the boat entirely out of the water and beached it glistening and dripping on its side against a bank of smooth boulders.

Behind the cement piling he prepared a fire of twigs and pine needles. When it came to a blaze, he added bits of driftwood, the larger pieces collected in the pine grove on the other side of the cove he broke on his knee. From the picnic basket she drew out ears of corn, a bottle of relish, mustard, a bag of chips, cellophane-packaged frankfurters and a plastic container of fresh tomatoes.

He pulled off his shirt, slipped out of his trousers and waded into the water.

Come in for a swim.

I should put the corn on the fire. They take a while to cook.

She made her way carefully along the red rock hugging the unshucked corn close to her body. She soaked them several minutes under water then pulled them out to drain on the rock.

He swam out and disappeared around the cliff. She followed the sounds he made swimming. Splashes, churns, gasps of air. Then a silence. He is probably swimming under water. She gathered up the wet corn and walked over to the crackling, devouring fire, flames weaving, falling, darkening, leaping. He will never come up again. She heard smooth rhythmical strokes, his body heaving then parting the water. She wrapped each ear of corn with leaves still intact in aluminum foil and closed the seams securely before throwing them on the fire. She stretched out on the pebbles, her toes touched water, her back bare to the sun. She heard him wade out of the water.

Marry me.

She half-turned her head, squinting her eyes to see him against the light.

Why?

Because I love you.

Because of the baby?

Marry me and have the baby.

She lowered her head on the rock and closed her eyes. He picked red pebbles from the beach and placed them loosely spaced in a circle around her.

Marry me. Don't go away.

I need to go away. I can't help him because I can't agree with him. He wills a change that in the end will destroy me. Before I leave you must help me bring my trees to his garden.

She cried in her wall of pebbles.

The crack of a gun echoed across the lake. End of the race. Time to go back and pack the few things she had brought along. She stepped out of his pebbled circle, tore open the cellophane-wrapped frankfurters and tossed them on top of the corn in the fire.

When they had finished eating he poured cupfuls of water on the fire.

The lake was a sheen of gold encircled by dark shores. The dark scattered islands loomed out of the water like petrified sentinels. In the distance she saw a moving haze, a cloud of locusts hovering above water.

What is it?

He brought the canoe to the edge of a watery field of wild rice, the tips just beginning to emerge above water, and halted there. With a sudden powerful scoop and a sharp twist of the paddle he entered the field. The canoe plowed a swift straight furrow through the center of the field, beating down the feathery stalks. Beneath the surface of the water flashing by, she saw stalks extending deep into the silent dark, the utter depths of the lake where she could not follow, the roots of stalks feeding and growing there.

*A*mah do I imagine it stirring that coiled warmth inside one cannot have child in retreat sweet that other life a part of me alive and growing with each tick of time. Unhook linen dress spotlessly washed clean by spray and sun brush hair put on powder to cover two dark pockets under the eyes.

The telephone rings.

I am well Dyadya. How are you? How is the market? Going away for the weekend? Are you staying in town just for your shadow boxing lessons?

Yes, the last lesson, must stay for the last lesson. Mr. Li so keen. His favorite pupil. Besides, Ngmah wants to stay in town. Tired, heat in town, market tired, everyone gone. When are you leaving? Come downtown and have lunch with me next week.

I'd love to.

Yes, we will lunch next week. Just put in an order to buy Steel in your account. Pays a good dividend which you will need while you're away. It might even make a move toward end of summer. If not don't worry we can always sell for year-end tax loss. You have made enough profit for the first six months. Do you agree?

Yes.

Everything will be taken care of.

Thank you.

We'll have lunch next week.

Yes. Sorry to hear you have to stay in town.

Don't want to disappoint Mr. Li. Don't like to disappoint anyone. Good-bye. Take care of yourself.

Good-bye Dyadya.

I love you. Go out and plant your trees, and water your flowers with powerful agile hands that made wounds and healed the wounded, planted trees and smashed the china, shaded exposed seedlings from the sun's ray, protected roots from predatory animals. There are two gates in the north wall, three in the south, two in the east and two in the west. Winds blow from all sides. In the center is stillness. Winds blow from all sides. The gates are open. The center shifts.

Sweet, that other part of me stirring. Unhook the dress. Pick up the ringing telephone.

Almost forgot to tell you. Someone I want you to meet before you go away. Excuse me as I do not know too much about these things but am willing to try because you are my daughter.

What is it?

Young man from Singapore I want you to meet.

Oh? Why?

Chinese. In banking and has our name. Our name, same name.

What do you mean?

I mean you don't have to change your name. You can keep it forever. I may be wrong but I figure it's what you want, isn't it? Great idea. Same name, same interests. How about that? You'll get along beautifully and your children will have your name.

Oh Dyadya for heaven's sake I haven't even met him yet. Besides I can't.

Why not?

Haven't the time. I'm leaving in a week.

Of course you have time. Meet him. I am your father and you are precious to me. For your own good. And we can all do banking together. You'll enjoy it I know you'll enjoy it. It's a wonderful idea. I am very excited.

No.

No? Your sisters have children and all of them I have endowed with trusts. Don't you want me to do the same for yours? Trust me. Trust me.

Thank you Dyadya, that's very kind of you.

About time you also got married. Then you needn't go away. We'll all do banking together. Trusts for all the children. You won't have to go away because you'll like him, I am almost certain. Besides, no harm meeting.

Thank you Dyadya, that's very kind of you.

Yes, yes, I know I made a mistake with the last one. Definitely not for you. This one is for you. Your sisters chose for themselves but in your case we can improve the choice by choosing together. Listen to me. This one is really different. Trust me and there'll be no regrets. No regrets. I shall be happy when you're settled, like all the others.

I have a lot of packing to do but perhaps I'll find time. . . .

Parting word. Your grandfather knew his father. Great chums in their youth. I know that will mean something to you . . .

I have to go now. Next week . . .

. . . And you might consider that in a way we are almost related.

Yes Dyadya. Good-bye.

Hello? I am sure you will not leave when you have met him. Next week then. Good-bye and take care of yourself.

Good-bye.

Her body was covered with sweat thick enough to peel. A gnawing lust seized her which only crabs could satisfy, the kind split in halves raw and left to soak in deep brown earthen jars, soaking in brine spiked with rice wine or sauteed in halves with sherry and ginger and fresh green scallions slightly browned sprinkled in thick golden sauce.

Days turned cold, the full moon came. It is supper-time and instead of eating by themselves with silent observant amahs standing in each corner of the room waiting upon the children's dining room they are seated in the main dining room around the heavy Western-styled rectangular table supported on smooth squared legs shorn of decoration the dark wood gleaming in the dim room, shades drawn over bay windows to keep out the noon and summer's heat when Ngmah took her daily English lesson, sitting erect at the table facing Miss Ironside the local protestant missionary. A glass of chilled grape juice diluted by melting ice stood by Miss Ironside's open book, another glass near Ngmah's right elbow. They read *Lady Windermere's Fan* in a blue cloth edition with titles printed in gold script.

But tonight indoors is cool as outdoors. In the dining room the blazing double tiered chandelier hovers over the white linen covered table and swallows perch on bare branches of trees flatly silhouetted against a round orange moon. They bring the steaming cauldron brim-ming with red white crabs, crusted uppersides red, ribbed undersides white, sharp white red claws thrust out stiffly, moist hairs matted on the edge of the underbelly shields. Each place is set with large plate and small sauce dish. At either end of the table, clustered among small dishes of precious gold soya sauce and vinegar, are dishes heaped with ginger sliced like match sticks chef's kitchen staff must have spent hours sharpening knives for slicing ginger, for slitting throats of chickens hanging by the feet head down dripping blood from the gash in the throat into shallow basins, collecting each drop for blood puddings, soft brown cubes floating in clear chicken broth.

Dyadya takes a crab, Ngmah takes a crab, amahs step forward to pick out crabs to put in plates of children. They bend their heads to concentrate on the hot crabs. Break them apart while still piping hot. Eat them fast enough so that the ones remaining in the cauldron should not get cold. Best hot. No noise except cracking and tearing shells apart, chewing, sucking. You're big enough to mix your own blend of soya sauce, vinegar, ginger, sugar to your liking. Plop. Watchful amahs empty the mess from the plates. Of a hundred different ways to eat crabs this is the best, stirs the heart and is the most basic. Do not invite guests. There are no outsiders attending the feast. They are eating at home among themselves.

Crabs diminish in the cauldron. They toss hollow shells and discard membranes into another bowl, a crazy growing heap of empty shells. That tasty stuff neither flesh nor egg nor membrane caked in the two extremities of the shell dig out with your nails from the tightest corners, a test of crab-eating proficiency.

The air seeping through closed windows tickles damp fingers and cools the few uneaten crabs in the bottom of the cauldron. It is all over. Amahs bring steaming white towels to wipe face and sticky fingers. Mouths sore and aching, tongues bruised from intricate maneuvers separating flesh from shell and cartilage. Clear the table, bring more towels, whoever not yet fulfilled and will not give up takes a last cold crab from the cauldron. Wipe hands and face Oh Lord God heart hand mouth in me With faith with hope with charity That I may run rise rest with Thee.

Amahs bring scalding ginger tea on trays in tall heavy glasses. Slices of fresh ginger float or rest on the bottom of glasses. Grasp the smooth glass near the rim so as not to burn the fingers. Add sugar and stir with a long-handled spoon. Caution! Fruits? Persimmon is death after crab. Drink the ginger tea while still hot. Yes, a pomegranate, have a pomegranate which you don't really like because it is hard and bitter to eat you want something soft and mushy like a persimmon especially after crab. Amah says death waits for you in the moonlit night if you eat persimmons after feast of crabs. Not to look even at a persimmon. Hide them.

She would take a bus and find her way to that restaurant which he had discovered where they served crabs, a very small hard shelled variety, she had to have them, covered with sticky ginger sauce. I am taking you for a long ride she said to the life inside her buttoning up the front of her linen dress.

*T*hough it was past the normal lunch period she was not the only diner. In the far end of the room next to the kitchen sat four young men. Their leather jackets hung on wall hooks above their booth. She had sat in that same booth one day she came with Dyadya and Ngmah and Seventh Jill home from school. In the middle of the meal she saw a cockroach crawl out of a crack between the upholstery and the wall where the leather jackets now hung. It climbed up the wall to the height of her elbow resting on the formica table top. Then everyone else noticed and stopped eating to watch in silent fascination the progress of the roach which slowly descended from the wall and just as slowly invaded the table. It disappeared under a plate to emerge and again disappear under more plates till it neared Dyadya's place at the outer edge of the table. Suddenly he picked up a menu lying on a table across the aisle and quick as lightning brushed the roach from the rim of his plate. He replaced the menu and continued eating, as they all did, pretending that nothing had happened.

She sat down at a table facing the bald owner who stood behind a counter recording lunch receipts in a green paged ledger. The waiter took her order, went into the kitchen and yelled out the order in the heavy accents of Southern seamen. There followed noise of quick chopping, an explosion of melting fat and frantic stirrings in the kitchen.

Sweat broke out over her body. She was hungry but forced down a desire to hurry into the kitchen to check how chef was making out with her crabs. The waiter brought the platter of crabs, shells separate from the innards, drowned in thick, shiny sauce. With the crabs came a bowl of rice and a pot of tea. She chewed into a crab and felt like throwing up. She poured tea into the small heavy china cup and took a sip. It was lukewarm and tasted bitter. She made another attempt with the crabs. The corners inside the shells were empty. Nothing to dig out. She spotted her dress in the front.

The crab feast was their very last it seemed, because soon after corpses floated on the river and under the wooden bridge which connected the kitchen courtyard and the cane fields. They did not cross the bridge or dig out the ling from the mud by the river bank. Gardeners spent an afternoon painting black the white walls encircling the grounds. All the while painting they peered anxiously at the cloudless sky.

She lost her hunger, paid her bill and went out into the hot street. She hailed a cab and arrived just on time at the doctor's office.

For the first time since they met they were walking together in broad daylight on the open street. They had spent the afternoon at her apartment and then had gone out to see a film. That morning when she telephoned his office he had taken the call right away for he had not heard from her for over a week while she was away from the city. Would he like to come tomorrow or the day after? He had hemmed and hawed, had started to say today but swallowed the word midway. She had picked him up on that and a half hour later he was at her door.

They parted soon after the end of the film. The lights had come on and evening traffic moved heavily in the streets. He had not said earlier what time he would leave and she considered it a further good sign when he hurried across the street to buy an evening paper that he might want to come home and read. He stood a few feet away from the newspaper stand, opened the paper and began to read. Read at my place. No he would be late for an appointment. He had to be on the other side of town by seven.

She started to walk anywhere to still her disappointment. He stopped her. Let's walk to the Circle. He would take the bus there. She had been walking in the direction of home but stopped short and turned his way. On second thought if she liked he would walk her home. No she would walk him to the Circle. She looked straight ahead as she walked. He followed a pace behind to watch her walk. She played absentmindedly with the fringe of her scarf. When they arrived at the Circle he suddenly smiled and became quite jovial. See you soon and he kissed her on both cheeks. He would probably call her the next day and they could meet on Saturday. No he wouldn't want to mark all this down because the pages of his calendar were crowded with all sorts of appointments related to his work. In any case he would telephone before Saturday. But look here he would be late for his appointment.

Would she like to walk him to his office? No she would rather go home. They turned away from each other at the same time. She took ten paces toward home when all at once she spun around and cried out his name. Laughing he retraced his steps. What is it? When will he call? Look that won't do at all. Can he call in the morning? Impossible.

She reached up and pulled together the lapels of his coat and buttoned them under the collar. He would catch cold. Would he call her at noon if he couldn't call her in the morning. She searched in her mind the word promise in his language, and failing, grasped him by the shoulders, reached up and kissed him on both cheeks. Then she turned and made her way back as if in dream waited while noiseless traffic sped by for the light to change at the intersection. The light changed. She shook away her daze, crossed the street and entered the house. She took her suitcases out of the closets and began to pack for the return trip home.

*G*randfather practices calisthenics. In the yard of his former gate keeper's house he makes studied movements of limbs and body. He is frail and each gesture is very precise. His eyes squint in the sun. His sight is clear. He retreats, advances, and with each change of movement he inhales and exhales. The air comes out of his mouth in puffs of vapor which dissolve in the morning air.

AFTERWORD

Originally published in 1968, *Crossings* preceded the first scholarly activity ever devoted to Asian American literature by five years. Thus its appearance was unheralded, and it went quickly out of print. Nonetheless, Chuang Hua's novel is a major landmark in Asian American literature.

A precursor of Maxine Hong Kingston's *The Woman Warrior, Crossings* reflects the influence of Flaubert, Hemingway, Faulkner, and the imagist poets. As such, it is Asian America's first modernist novel. Experimental in structure and form, the fragmented narrative is a collage of dreams, nightmares, autobiography, and fantasy. Its prose is often elegantly spare, its punctuation and syntax often unconventional. Quotation marks may be omitted; fragments and run-on sentences abound, and characters are often referred to only by pronoun. Spatial and temporal settings are unspecified, and chronological leaps may occur even within a single paragraph. Still, internal clues and final revelations ultimately enable the reader to see the picture whole.

As Louis Chu's *Eat a Bowl of Tea* has been considered the most authentic literary rendering of the Chinese American lower-middle-class male social milieu, so *Crossings* is the fullest expression of the upper-class female émigré experience. The shifting world of its protagonist, a dislocated Chinese American woman named Fourth Jane, is figured by this central image:

> She stood in the center of the square carpet of faded reds greens and blues and whites in which she discerned oases and deserts, scorpions and camels, departures, wanderings and homecomings woven inextricably there. (p. 187)

Though the story is framed by the beginning and end of her love affair with a Parisian journalist, it is concerned primarily with Fourth Jane's search for self. Fourth Jane *is* the figure in the carpet; its "faded reds greens and blues and whites" represent her childhood memories, while the "oases and deserts" suggest the gentler and harsher aspects of her experience. The "wanderings and homecomings" refer to myriad spatial and temporal crossings in Fourth Jane's life. These begin in childhood, when Fourth Jane moves with her parents from China to England and finally to the United States. As an adult she spends a long period in France. There are seven ocean crossings and four major cultural transitions, and the effect of these numerous dislocations is a rich experience of cultural diversity at the expense of a sense of centeredness.

Fourth Jane experiences dislocation on personal, familial, and even national levels, beginning with her position as the middle child in a family of seven, which calls upon her to fill two contradictory roles: She must be the responsible older child as well as the deferential and dependent younger sibling. And her Chinese name, Chuang Hua, suggests her parents' ambivalence about her femaleness and results in her own sense of inadequacy: "Chuang" distinguishes the boys in the family, and "Hua" is the name given to the girls.

Fourth Jane seeks a stable, unchanging center outside herself, and her parents' unity is the locus of her security, such as it is. Thus she feels her identity threatened when they disagree about Fifth James's marriage with a "barbarian," a Caucasian. Jane is shaken when her father backs off from his initial furious objection and goes to the hospital to visit his daughter-in-law and new grandson. Jane sides with her mother in remaining adamantly against the foreign intruder, but she anguishes over this split: "I feel a terrible danger crossing. The oneness of you and Ngmah you have built so tightly you can't undo overnight just to accommodate them" (p. 196–97). She feels she must separate from them for a time; as she explains, "I don't know who I am outside of the old context and I'm afraid I might not survive the new" (p. 196). And yet she goes away only to become involved with a "foreigner" herself.

China and America evoke similar, conflicting feelings in Fourth Jane. When her French lover tells her that she is equally an exile in America and in France, and that she should go back to China where she really belongs, she explains that she has loved both China and America, "as two separate but equal realities of my existence." And when the civil war in China and the Korean conflict between America and China preclude a return to China, she feels numb: "In that paralysis I lived in no man's land. . . . I had such longings to make a rumble in the silence. But both parts equally strong canceled out choice" (p. 122). Thus, on many levels, Fourth Jane experiences overwhelming conflicts, sufficiently powerful to produce emotional and physical torpor: "On certain days moving from one room to another in her apartment was the only displacement she felt capable of undertaking."

However, like the narrator in Kingston's *Woman Warrior*, Fourth Jane resolves these conflicts *through* her narrative. As she remembers her father after his death, she realizes that, though his power and smothering love were oppressive, his strength, talent, adaptability, ingenuity, and pride contributed much to the life of the family. Her mundane memories of him—planting beans at their country home, organizing endless rounds of birthday celebrations and family outings, and driving three hours to her college just to bring her a typewriter—help to create a coherent shape for her experience. As Chuang Hua demonstrates, it is in the simple tasks and responsibilities of living, as one recalls them or performs them, that wholeness and motivation may be found. The domestic chore of cooking is one of these, and Chuang Hua devotes many pages to the increasingly complex dinners that Fourth Jane prepares for her lover, from steak, to stuffed chicken, to Peking duck. These meals, an expression of love, are an affirmation of life in the face of confusion and depression.

Chuang Hua's synthetic vision and her acute sense of oppositions are also sharply realized in her most graphic images, which bring together the beautiful and the horrifying, the dignified and the absurd. Thus, "bloated corpses" that "flowed in the current of the yellow river" are juxtaposed with the "slenderest, reddest" stalks of sugar cane, "most tender and full of juice inside sweet to chew and suck on" (p. 49). And on one occasion, with great ceremoniousness and in order of rank, all the family members pay tribute to grandmother on her birthday, while she sits enthroned, muttering the only English words she can recall, "Machine gun" (p. 26). In another passage, a cotton sanitary pad soaks in a basin of bloody water on a white tiled floor beside a basket of "purple red lichees and yellow loquats" (p. 43). These disparate images, mixing decay and life, ugliness and beauty, horror and nourishment, reveal an unflinching, unrestrained vision, one that recognizes the harsh reality of coexisting opposites—"oases and deserts, scorpions and camels." As Chuang Hua reaches for artistic coherence through images, so Fourth Jane tries to achieve personal coherence, through her memories and her acceptance of everyday responsibilities.

Like other books by American ethnic minorities— Zora Neal Hurston's *Their Eyes Were Watching God* and Leslie Harmon Silko's *Ceremony* come to mind—*Crossings* is part of an important strain in American literature that insists upon the affirmation of difference and the reclaiming of origins. And yet, Chuang Hua's themes—crossing cultural barriers, crossing parental and conventional strictures, searching for a center within oneself from the past that is ever present—are not limited to Chinese Americans: rather, they are universal concerns.

Amy Ling

CHUANG HUA (the Chinese name and pen name of Stella Yang Copley) was born in Shanghai in 1931. During the Japanese invasion, she fled with her family to Hong Kong, eventually moving to England, and then to the United States, where she graduated from Vassar College in 1951. She lived a very private and reclusive life, refusing interviews and public recognition. Chuang Hua died on June 25, 2000. *Crossings* is her only known written work.

AMY LING, born in 1939, was the director of Asian American Studies at the University of Wisconsin-Madison when she passed away in 1999. A pioneer in her field, Ling published several books including *Chinamerica Reflections, Between Worlds: Women Writers of Chinese Ancestry, Reading the Literatures of Asian America, Imagining America: Stories from the Promised Land,* and *Yellow Light: The Flowering of Asian American Arts.*